ODDS-ON MURDER

ODDS-ON MURDER

JACK DOLPH

COACHWHIP PUBLICATIONS
Greenville, Ohio

To Sally

. . . who says, "All right, so it *isn't* the Great American Novel! It's *your* novel and it's got hard covers on it like anybody else's book."

Odds-On Murder, by Jack Dolph
© 2020 Coachwhip Publications edition

First published 1948
John ("Jack") Mather Dolph, 1895-1962
CoachwhipBooks.com

ISBN 1-61646-498-4
ISBN-13 978-1-61646-498-1

1

Street scene. Enter Katie . . .

"Hi, Doc!"

"Hi, Katie! What goes?"

"Lunch."

"Fine day for't."

"Yeah. Swell! See you around, Doc." Exit Katie.

Just like that.

So I am standing in my fine city suit at the corner of Forty-eighth and Broadway looking at Katie Storm's beautiful back. From the moment I'd crawled out at the brisk hour of five to eleven I'd known I was in for one of those days.

Into Rosie's for ham and eggs. The coffee was worse than usual and the *Herald Tribune* had syrup on it. The news wasn't much . . . International Affairs: Pete Mikchek, U. S. middleweight stops British champ in the sixth. Labor Front: Professional Baseball Guild declares something-or-other. Financial: Belmont Mutual Take tops two million. There was more but I gave it up. The normal routine of the morning just wouldn't go.

Somehow, every time the Storm girl shows me that competent looking back of hers, all the school teachers I ever had parade up and give out with their old familiar chorus . . . "James, you have such a good mind if you'd only *use* it!"

The hell of it is that all the school teachers seem to be wearing Katie's lively Irish face . . . and, brother, that makes teachers easy to look at in any man's league!

If I hadn't been a doctor, I'd have taken a shot of Eno and charged it off to a mild hangover. Or maybe if I *had* been a doctor . . . a real working doctor . . . I'd have been too busy with other people's troubles to be worrying about my own.

As it is, I am a doctor of sorts because my father was a doctor . . . of considerably more than sorts. Currently we have both retired, he at seventy-one and I . . . how old am I? Thirty-four. The Old Doc served in the other war and I have been out something over a year after fifty-two months in this one. For those four and a quarter years I was a real doctor. There was a lot to do and pretty often not much to do it with. It was mean, hard, exacting work but, in common with a lot of other guys, I got it done. I've got a cigar box full of stuff that tells what and where. The man didn't give me anything that tells why.

The Old Doc has a tendency to brag about it. He thinks my war must have been tougher than his. It's hard for him to understand that wars aren't big or little except on maps. When that man points that gun at you, mister, your war's as big as it can ever get.

Anyway, the Old Doc had his heart set on my being a physician, and a physician I am.

It's only on mornings like this that I think about really hanging out my shingle again or getting some gal to answer the telephone. I dislike what happens to doctors who invite all and sundry with signs, no matter how modest. I saw too much of that at home. I also dislike the inevitable attitude of office-girls and their ideas about the sanctity of appointments. My appointments are apt to be made, and not a few kept, in pleasant places like Bill Duffy's.

I have sort of an office . . . a pretty good one as a matter of fact. Last year, when everyone was looking for a place to live, I hit the daily double with two adjoining apartments and knocked a door in between. The other one is my office.

Needless to say, my practice is small and casual. It seems to have limited itself to patching up old ballplayers, fixing fighters' hands, spraying actors' throats and treating hangovers for sundry local characters.

More interesting, however, friends who train racehorses swear by me as an expert on gimpy legs and bucked shins. To this useless facet of my practice I am completely devoted.

For these services to humanity and equinity I do not generally get paid. On rare occasions of stress I send out bills and, surprisingly, receive money. Mostly I don't bother.

It seems well, here, to add for the more rational reader that my Uncle Will, a dissolute person who had little or no faith in my future as a physician, left me a modest income for life. Why, I don't know unless it was because I once socked Horace, his highly moral and disapproving son, on the nose. Perhaps it was because he worshiped the Old Doc.

So, you see? That's how it is. And, of course, that's why Katie Storm says "See you around, Doc," and shows me her beautiful back.

Ah, Katie, Katie, Katie!

I paid my check and left Rosie's blue as a pool-player's finger. On the way back to the apartment I kept wondering what I'd be like if I were different. Or does that make sense? I mean if I were . . . what do they call doctors when they get good? Eminent. That's it. If I were in the way of becoming eminent. "Dr. James Cardigan Connor, the eminent proctologist, is resting for a few days at Inner Springs."

Nuts!

However, Inner Springs reminded me of Willow Springs, Mister Fitz's fine colt running in the sixth race at Belmont and I stopped wondering about eminence and started wondering if I were too late to make the race-train.

2

All you have to do is stick around our teeming little neighborhood long enough and stuff happens to you. Either you get hit by a cab, altercate with obnoxious drunks or entertain some dope from home. Anyway, Forty-eighth Street is no place for a rocking chair and a good book.

Katie says it's what I get for hanging around with the ragtag and bang-tail . . . that if I had taken her advice in the first place and settled down on the East Side, like *people* do, all this would never have happened to me. She's particularly vocal on the subject.

It was this way.

Among my acquaintances around this end of town I number one John Joseph Burns. His proper name is Jocko. Now Burns makes a very good dollar out of advising certain of the well-heeled and otherwise unadvised gentry how to bet on the races. Jocko must not be confused with the hard-working fraternity of handicappers who get paid for their published selections . . . you know . . . "Associated Press: Wardroom, Fire King, Miss Kitty. United Press: Wardroom, Fire King, Miss Kitty. *Louisville Times:* Slapstick, Miss Kitty, Papa's Choice."

Burns is more likely to get paid for such statements as "Pass the race." These comments he issues from his modest office in the Paragon Building, at intervals, by telephone, by wire and by soft, convincing personal contacts. Occasionally people who have reason to refer to Jocko speak of him as a tout, but, in my opinion, touts are a breed of nickel-and-dime operators who aren't getting away with it and who have to spend a lot of time around the tracks hustling a living. Jocko is definitely getting away with it and is allergic to small bettors and horses alike. Small bettors give him nothing and horses, in the flesh, give him asthma. Exposure to either is equally objectionable to Jocko.

It was this John Joseph Burns who sounded my buzzer one night a few weeks ago and let me in for one of the damnedest messes you could imagine . . . one which almost sent me seeking the comfortable respectability of Beekman Place.

I was filing some X-rays after deciding there was nothing the matter with Hank Paulson's pitching arm except his wife's disposition. As a matter of fact, I had decided to haul out some new stuff on arthritis and spend the evening reading when the buzzer announced the end of my good intentions and the beginning of a lot of things that shouldn't happen to Hitler.

It was nine-thirty-five.

Jocko was calling from what we use for a lobby and he was in a sweat. His "Hey, Doc, lissen. Can I come up?" was out of character and sounded as though somebody was chasing him. I told him to come on up and got the whiskey and some ice from the kitchen as the elevator clanked its way to my floor. Jocko rapped and clumped in.

He's a big soft guy, with something the matter with his central nervous system . . . has an awkwardness that isn't natural. As he fumbled with his hat and coat he seemed more than ever physically confused. He wheezed like a leaky valve trying to get his wind, opening and closing his large, loose mouth with each gasp.

"Sit down, Jocko. Have a drink."

"Yeah, yeah. Thanks, Doc." He wedged himself in my reading chair and looked cornered. "Yeah, yeah. A drink would be fine."

I set the stuff in front of him and waited. It couldn't be money. Not if he came to me with it. Woman trouble was out of the question. In Burns' book a woman and a three-horse parlay represented about equal chances.

Before he spoke, Jocko wheezed himself through about a dollar's worth of my Old Forester and I figured it must be pretty bad because the big fellow's not much of a drinker . . . as drinkers go in this neighborhood. Finally it came out.

"Look, Doc, I'm in a hell of a jam."

"Tell me about it."

His heavy face—stamped with some Abie's Irish Rose romance of fifty-odd years ago—was dripping, lumpy, saffron.

"I run into something, Doc. Bad. I gotta have help. You're the only guy I know around that I can trust that much. That's why I came here."

"Sure, Jocko, you know I'll help you if I can . . ." Even then I sensed that maybe I was asking for something. "What's the trouble?"

"Plenty. You know Harry Lennen, don't you?"

I knew the guy casually and said so.

"Well, I just come from his room, Doc. He owed me some money, see, and I went up there to see him about it and . . ."

". . . and what?"

"He's dead. Somebody killed him. He's—jeez, Doc, he's all over the place!"

"What do you mean all over the place?" I had the quick, exciting impression the guy was putting on an act.

"His head! Somebody's bashed him over the head with something heavy. Goddamighty! There's blood and—stuff all over!"

"You just walked in on him?"

"Yeah. I rapped, see? Harry didn't answer—"

"—and the door was unlocked?"

"The door was unlocked so I just went in."

"Why?"

Jocko squirmed a little. Maybe not too much. "I know him pretty well and I thought maybe he was—you know—drunk or something. I figured if his door was unlocked he'd be around there somewhere."

"Sure. When was that, Jocko?"

"Just now, Doc. I just come from there."

I looked at my watch. It was nine-forty. "Tell me. How long were you in the room?"

"Only just long enough to see what I seen and get the hell out of there." Burns' color was coming back and he was getting his breathing under some sort of control. I'd learned all I was going to learn from him because of his excitement. He must have been in a pretty bad way when he arrived. He's usually a hard man under pressure. Nine-forty. Five minutes here, maybe five minutes on the way and a couple of minutes, more or less, there. With his hurry, possibly ten minutes would cover it all.

"How long had Lennen been dead?"

"Jeez! How would I know, Doc?"

"Was the body cold? Or stiff?"

"I don't know. I . . ."

"How about the blood? Was it dried?"

"I didn't go near him. I like to threw up as it was."

"I suppose so."

What am I—a detective or something? I keep asking the guy questions instead of calling the cops. Yet there's something about Jocko that makes me go on with it. There's something about this thing that is trying to ring a bell in the back of my mind. If I don't ask the rest of the questions now they'll never be answered. At least that's the way I feel about it.

"Was the light turned on in Lennen's room? Or did you turn it on?"

"Lessee." Jocko was ponderous with thought. "Lessee. It *had* to be on, Doc, I didn't touch no light switch and I seen him plain enough. The light was on."

"I see. Did you look around long enough to see what he had been killed with. The weapon?"

"No. Nothing like that. Like I told you, I just took one look and beat it."

"That's natural enough. I can't say I blame you. Tell me, Jocko, did you see anyone around the place?"

"I didn't see anybody special. Some people were in the street of course. Nobody I knew."

"Then you'd guess that nobody saw you?"

"God! I hope not! You know how that place is at night."

"What place?"

"Fifty-third Street, Doc. Next to where the old Rhythm Club used to be. It's an old three-story apartment building. Harry had the second floor. You know the place?"

"I think so." At least I knew the old Rhythm Club well enough. Since they'd closed, that block would be pretty well deserted at nine-thirty—dark and quiet except for the clatter of bowling pins from the big alleys near by. Well, that was about all of it. I figured I might as well get to the point.

"You call the cops?"

"Well, no, Doc. I was kinda excited and all that and . . . that's why I come here right away. I thought maybe . . ."

"Sure, Jocko, you thought maybe I'd find some way to let the police know about it . . . and keep you out of it. Right?"

"Something like that I s'pose. I hadn't figured it out exactly. You make it sound kind of tough. You being so well liked around here and all that . . ." The big guy was wallowing in it.

"You aren't in any trouble with the law, are you, Jocko?" I couldn't help adding, "Any other trouble?"

Burns did another immense squirm. "No. No real trouble but just right now the cops ain't healthy for me . . . with making a little handbook on the side and all that. You know how it is."

"Just that? Nothing else?"

"That's all. Nothing that amounts to anything, but I can't afford to tangle with no police with Harry owing me dough like he did. It wouldn't look good."

"I'll say it wouldn't!"

The big slob looked like he was about to cry. I suppose I was sorry for him or something. Perhaps it was because, as I looked at the guy, I was certain he'd never smashed Lennen's skull. Whatever it was, it wasn't my native common sense. I've got nobody but myself to blame. Jocko's story smelled like the Fulton Market. Even if he had told me the truth about everything I'd asked him, there was something wrong. The old warning bells rang in the back of my head and everything about the thing suggested that I run like hell.

Yet, somehow, I knew that, before the night was over, I'd be into it up to my neck.

"One more thing," I heard myself saying, "did you touch anything in the room? Anything at all?"

"God no, Doc, I remembered about that. I was careful."

So he remembered about that! He was careful, was he? I asked him how about the doorknob and he leered like a punch-drunk fighter. "I wiped that off."

"You did."

"Yeah. With my hankychiff." Pleased as a bum at a free lunch. I didn't say anything for a while, so he poured himself another drink.

"Jocko."

"What, Doc?"

"As I understand it, you want me to go up there, discover the body, report the murder and say I just wandered in to pass the time of day."

"You could do that, couldn't you, without getting into any trouble?"

"Maybe. Maybe not. That depends. But there's another thing."

"Yeah?"

"Yeah. Why do you want me to go up there at all?"

Jocko looked into his drink as though he'd found a fly in it, then back at me. "I don't getcha."

"I'll put it plainly. Why are you so anxious to have the body discovered by somebody—especially by me?"

He looked into all his mental pockets like a man who's lost his wallet—then gave it up. "I dunno, Doc. It seemed like somebody had to find him sooner or later and maybe you was the guy to do it."

Well, well, well! Right in my lap. A peachy chance to play cops-'n'-robbers. Okay, chump, go right up there and walk into a room full of cops. Or, if you're lucky, take a look-see and get caught later.

"Well, I'll tell you, Jocko, I'll play it this far with you. I'll forget all about your coming here tonight unless somebody downtown finds out about it . . . or knows about it now . . . and faces me with it. Then I'll stall the best I can. Beyond that I won't promise anything."

"You won't . . . go up there?"

"I'd be a damned fool to go up there and you know it. But I'll keep you out of it if anything's said to me . . . that is, I'll keep you out of it as long as I can. I'll even cut a corner or two for you because I'm fool enough to believe your story . . . most of it, anyway. But if you've got any bigger stake in this thing than you've told me, God help you. I'll have you down at Police Headquarters right now! Get that straight. If you've got anything more to tell me, spill it because you'll be in a hell of a spot if you don't . . . to say nothing of the spot *I'll* be in."

I got a tremendous, whiskey-laden wheeze in the face that must have been a sigh of relief. "You can be sure I had nothing to do with it, Doc. Nothing at all."

After a while, Jocko rumbled down in the elevator and was gone. I put away the whiskey and finished filing the X-rays. I don't know why I was stalling. I knew perfectly well that I was going to walk into something . . . and when I'd walked into it, I wasn't going to like any part of it.

3

I locked up and headed for Fifty-third Street.

Harry Lennen had been one of those social and economic mysteries you find only in big towns. Nobody knew much about him and, as nearly as I had ever heard, nobody gave much of a damn except, possibly, Terry Hale, a local taxi-dancer with whom he'd been seen around a lot.

Lennen had been neither a useful, nor even a tolerable member of society—even in our neighborhood where nobody pays much attention to you so long as you stay out of jail and none at all if you don't. He had been a hanger-on—a parasite who fed on other parasites. Onetime sheet-writer and runner for the book-makers and general errand lad for the fight crowd and such, Harry had outsmarted himself. His petty grifting and, what's worse with that crowd, his loose tongue had landed him in a spot where it must have been pretty rough for him to hustle a buck for himself around the town. Any one of a hundred guys—and a few women—could have hit him over the head without much compunction and with little or no loss to the citizenry.

I'm afraid, however, that my good but serious friend, Eddie Marsh, of the New York Police Department, wouldn't look at it that way. The capable lieutenant is a sworn and professional enemy of people who violently destroy our citizens, regardless of the worth of the destroyees.

My own worthlessness is a favorite topic of Eddie's. In that respect, Eddie is sort of a male Katie, joining her in periodic and gleeful campaigns for my reform. I am sincerely fond of the big cop, but sometimes I dread to see him coming down the street. Certainly my present errand wasn't going to help that situation much and, as I turned into Seventh Avenue, my stomach started back home.

Somehow I spurred the unwilling flesh into Fifty-third Street and reconnoitered the ground. There was the usual number of moving cars in the street, mostly cabs, but none parked in the immediate vicinity of the apartment. As I walked briskly past on the far side of the street I checked the lights. Somebody was home on the third floor but the lights were out on the first. I couldn't see a sign of the light Jocko had said he'd left burning in the Lennen flat on the second . . . but didn't worry about it because even a careless murderer doesn't leave bodies on the second floor of a New York building with the shades up.

I walked back to Seventh and crossed the street. If anyone came along I'd pass the place and try it again. If not, this was it. It seemed reasonable to believe that, if the body had been discovered, there would be cops and lights and cars all over the place. My ears made sirens out of any sounds that came along as I neared the steps. Nobody around. I went up as though I belonged there. Like an ass, I had forgotten my gloves. I opened the downstairs door with a handkerchief. The door was loose, badly fitted. Like it hadn't been locked for years.

The hall was lighted by a dirty bulb and smelled of old things—the second-hand smells that accumulate in a building where too many people have lived too many years. I stepped carefully past the door of the ground floor apartment and tried the first step. The expected creak startled me—others exploded behind me all the way up to the landing. Then there was the door. Another dirty bulb showed the cheap metal 2. It also showed an open transom behind which there was no light.

Okay, Connor, you asked for it. Somebody has been here since Jocko Burns. Maybe he's left—and maybe he's in there waiting for you. Or waiting for somebody. Or just waiting to see what happens. Never mind those bells ringing in the back of your mind, just go right on in. If the situation gets really dangerous we'll send up a rocket.

I knocked softly on the door. Silence. I said, "Harry. Are you home?" It sounded like somebody else's voice and scared me worse than the silence. I rapped again. Said my speech again. Silence. That didn't mean anything, of course, and I licked an impulse to leg it down the stairs and out of there.

I put my handkerchief over the doorknob and turned it a little. The door was unlocked and started to open inward with the weight of my hand. I let it go and stepped back. Silence and darkness beyond. My covered hand groped the door frame and found the reassuring projection of tumbler switch . . . flipped it.

Between getting through the door, getting it closed behind me and knocking over a small stand I damned near scared myself to death.

But there it was. Jocko Burns hadn't been kidding about that, anyway. Harry Lennen was as dead as people ever get. How long he'd been dead some smarter guy than I will have to tell you. Maybe an hour or so. The M.E. would have it down to the minute for the morning papers.

I looked around. Lennen had lived, and died, in a hole. The thing inhaled through a grimy window from the doubtful air of Fifty-third and exhaled through the bedroom into God knows what behind the building. There was also a tiny aperture in the can.

The place was a mess. Nothing broken or anything like that, just a routine mess. Empty cans, dirty underwear and cigarette butts. If there were what the reporters like to call "signs of a struggle" it was the struggle for existence.

Harry lay in a nasty heap on the floor . . . the sort of pile people fall into when they go out standing up. Disorderly. There was no doubt of the fact that somebody, as Jocko had said, had "hit him with something." Whoever did it wasn't fooling around. The police surgeon would call it multiple fractures, but, between you and me, it didn't need any diagnosing. I didn't bother to touch the wound but looked around for the weapon that could have caused such a mess.

It was there, of course—chucked aside as casually as though the killer had been a slaughterhouse employee gone to lunch. It was nothing fancy—nothing that meant anything—just a quart milk bottle. There were others, dirty ones, in the bedroom. This one looked as if it had been rinsed and used for coffee. There was a coffee-like stain in the bottom and a drop or two, still liquid inside. The bottle was decorated with ample evidence of its violent and lethal use and was destined to become The People's Exhibit A—the "murder weapon."

Harry Lennen's execution had been a mean, violent and purposeful one. The weight of the bottle precluded any guess as to the sex of the killer. Anyone who could lift the thing could have killed with it. The man's head showed that he had been hit repeatedly. It's a pretty good bet, however, that the first blow killed him because of the nature of the damage. The whole thing was indescribably vicious and brutal—yet it could have been done by a woman. Of course I thought of Terry Hale. Yes, it could have been done by a woman who was fit enough to jitterbug with fifty guys a night. I'd seen her around and she had hardly seemed the sort to do a thing like this. I guess most of the people who do . . . don't.

I left the bottle where it had fallen—at the end of the couch. The glass surface would be swell for prints.

Even there on the floor, Harry Lennen looked more prosperous than I had ever seen him. His hands and nails were clean, a violent departure from his custom. He wore a neat, blue suit and a new looking tie of conservative pattern. His shirt, where I could see its original color, was blue-gray and clean. His shoes were new. Two pair in the bedroom were broken and disreputable. Harry either had been places or was expecting to visit some.

Carefully I went through his pockets and found the usual stuff. A money clip holding a laundry claim check and a dollar bill. Some loose silver. In his breast pocket a few natural odds and ends and a letter from Terry Hale suggesting Harry return the money he had borrowed and be quick about it. She needed it and she knew he had it. His life was his own and she hadn't any kick about the way he led it. It wasn't the brush-off she minded so much as the fact that he thought he could go his merry way owing her dough. Cordially, Terry Hale. Cordially, eh?

Strange a dame as wise as La Belle Hale should have lent the bum money in the first place. Stranger still that she thought she stood a chance of getting it back. I left the letter.

There didn't seem to be much else for me to see. Maybe somebody like Lieutenant Eddie Marsh could have read a volume into it—maybe not. It looked to me as though the guy was going along in a semi-normal sort of way when somebody got sore at him and bopped him with the first thing that came to hand. Yes, and kept bopping him until the people downstairs must have thought Lennen was building something.

I hadn't looked into the clothes-closet. There might be something there. I went into the bedroom again to have a look and turn off the light before I left.

Back in my head the bell rang again. I stopped. I hadn't been paying enough attention to that bell. Warning. Of what? Of the fact that the clothes-closet door was standing open. It had been closed when I'd been in the bedroom before. I turned to look behind the half-open door back of me . . .

Then the promised rocket went off. The walls, the ceiling and the floor appeared before me in rapid succession as a possible place to lie down. I apparently chose the floor. At least that's what I was trying to push out of my face a while later. There was quite a lot of engineering to getting up and the problem kept me busy for some time. The bedroom light was out and I had no desire whatever to turn it on again. Through the door I could see the living room and the way out of there. Operation scram took precedence over all other personal activity and I set out.

A series of weaving maneuvers got me to the hall door. The problem of whether to leave the lights on or off was too much for me. I left them off as I'd found them, smudged the door handle with my handkerchief and staggered down the stairs without caring much if I made a racket.

The street seemed clear. Nobody standing around and nothing unusual in the way of parked cars or traffic. I headed out and didn't look back. At Seventh Avenue I went into the drug store and called the cops. As distinctly as I could I said, "There's been a murder," and gave the address. That was all.

As I passed the Roxy I heard the sirens. By the time I had closed my apartment door and flopped into my couch I knew that Harry Lennen's apartment was being tramped over by the crew of a radio car. By the time I had lugged my bulk to the kitchen and made myself a drink I knew that a highly trained team of experts were setting out to build a chain of facts that would drag somebody to the electric chair.

My head ached and I went to bed hoping they wouldn't put Eddie Marsh on the case.

But of course they did.

4

It had to happen sooner or later, but I had twenty-four hours to think it over before the cops got around to me. At that, I wasn't much further along when Eddie called me. The whole thing had paraded through my mind endlessly without result. Maybe it was as simple as it looked. If so, Terry or Jocko would get thrown in the jug and that would be that.

Then who hit me over the head? And with, incidentally, what? Not that it made much difference with the case but it was no pillow and I was curious. Whoever the guy was he didn't care to be seen around the corpse. I couldn't blame him for that. It could have been Terry Hale. It even could have been Jocko . . . there was time enough. Hell! It could have been Billy the Oysterman.

No, it wasn't simple as it worked out. But then you'd know that. You'd know that I wouldn't be sitting here sweating out reams of this guff which Katie swears will be a book unless it was nice and mysterious. You could have fooled me, anyway.

So the phone rang and there was Eddie . . . Eddie on business than which there can be nothing businesser. I don't know yet whether it was because he knew something or just because I was a friend who gets around a little in this end of town.

"Doc," he had said, "what do you know about Harry Lennen?"

I had a panicky moment trying to unscramble the things I knew about Lennen then and what I'd known twenty-four hours before.

Marsh gave me time to think by adding, "As you've no doubt heard because of the company you choose to keep, somebody murdered him last night. Frankly, we haven't much to go on."

Eddie sounded too smug for the words he was saying. I've played poker with him enough to recognize that pat manner. Maybe it was just his regular professional technique. Not having played cops-'n'-robbers with him, I wouldn't know.

So I told him what I knew about Lennen. I'd taken care of him once when he thought he was sick and said so. I told Eddie as much as I could about the guy's disorderly life . . . that he owed everybody money most of the time and that sort of thing.

"You haven't heard of his getting hold of any money recently, have you, Doc? Maybe quite a lot?"

"No, I haven't . . . but then I never saw much of him around, I wouldn't know if he'd got hold of a lot of money or not. Why?"

"We were just a little curious, down here, to know where Lennen would get ten nice, clean one-thousand-dollar bills . . . all crisp and new, right out of the bank!" I wasn't too surprised to notice that the good lieutenant was enjoying that morsel. "We found it neatly sewn in the lining of his coat."

"Ten grand on that tramp? That's a lot of dough."

"Yes, Doc, that's a lot of dough. Would you have any ideas?"

The voice of Jocko Burns wheezed through my mind . . . "Harry owes me some dough . . . wouldn't look good." I'd have given a pretty to know that Eddie wasn't playing games with me. I had a strong hunch he was, but I told him I wouldn't have any ideas and added some asinine crack like wasn't that amazing.

"We thought it was, Doc."

I was relieved when Eddie didn't follow it up too hard and finally got off into the amenities that men can't seem to leave out of telephone calls . . . why don't we have lunch someday soon and that sort of thing. I hung up, plenty puzzled.

Ten grand! . . . ten thousand dollars on that bum! Probably in a neat, flat package. Sewn in the lining of his thirty-five-dollar Sunday suit. That didn't make sense. Or did it?

Certainly that much money didn't say anything about Terry Hale. It could have said a lot about Jocko Burns, however, and

I looked up the number of his hotel. It was too late for him to be around the horse-rooms and I might catch him. I did.

"This is Doc, Jocko."

"Yeah, Doc, I see where . . ."

"Don't talk, listen. How much did you try to collect from our friend the other night?"

"What friend, Doc?" Bland as that. What the hell! I'd better shake this guy up. He's all set to walk out and leave me with most of the mess in my lap. Certainly he wouldn't act that way unless he knew I had gone to Lennen's apartment. My skull reminded me somebody knew.

"This is no time for stalling, Burns. The guy I'm talking about is the one you say you found dead in . . ."

"Wait a minute, Doc . . . not over the phone . . . I just . . ."

"Okay. Don't make me draw pictures then. How much did he owe you?"

"Not much. I forget the exact amount . . . just a little deal I had with him. There's nothing to do but forget it, now."

By this time there's not much doubt in my mind about what's going on. Any time Jocko Burns starts forgetting how much people owe him you can start selling off your bonds and start buying canned food. The end of the dollar is in sight.

"Nothing to do about it but forget it?" I told him, "There may be a hell of a lot to do about it before you get clear of this. There are some reasonably smart guys downtown, including Eddie Marsh, who are trying to find out where this punk got ten thousand dollars in new bills. Maybe you can help me on that!"

That put the big guy back in form. He wheezed quite naturally again and spluttered, "So he had . . . he had the . . . where was it, Doc? Where did they find it?"

I had to laugh . . . and did. This fellow would grab a twenty off a high-tension power line.

"Sure he had it . . . had it all the time. Sewn in the lining of his best suit. It was right there while you were looking at him, Jocko, right there under your hand. He had the bills down in the lining toward his pocket so the block wouldn't show. It was big as a Hershey bar . . . and you missed it when you searched him, pal. Too bad because nobody knew he had that dough . . . except maybe you."

He was still spluttering when I hung up. I had the uncomfortable feeling that, sooner or later, I might have to explain why I hadn't found the bills myself.

Ten thousand dollars is a lot of money. Not only is it a lot of money to be found on a penniless hanger-on in this neck of the sporting woods but even among the wise percentage boys up and down the street. Sure, you hear of hundred-thousand-dollar bets being made on horses and fights, and many have been. But they are mostly fable. I get around pretty much with the aces in that line and I couldn't tell you where you could place that kind of a bet . . . certainly not where you'd have any assurance of getting paid if you won.

I'm pretty certain the bills that Harry Lennen had to part with so violently hadn't been betting money. No wise head like Jocko Burns would have been fool enough to pick Lennen as a betting commissioner . . . or even as a messenger. He was completely untrustworthy and, worse, he talked too much.

What then? There was no question of Jocko's being messed up in the thing someplace . . . the ten thousand if not the killing. No question, either, of Harry's getting it in any legitimate way. He just didn't. It might have been a lot of things . . . blackmail, ransom, bribery by messenger or just plain stealing.

Whoever killed him either didn't know about the money, didn't know he had it, or was scared off while he was looking for it. It seemed easier to believe that Lennen had been killed for some reason associated with the money, but not for the money itself. That would make sense. He gets tangled up in some deal involving the payment of ten thousand dollars . . . certainly not from him or to him . . . and whoever's on the wrong end of the deal knocks him off with no idea, possibly, of getting his dough back.

Even ten stiff, new bills make quite a hunk of stuff to wear around in the lining of a coat. He couldn't have had the money too long . . . not there, at least, because he would have been wearing his best suit every day. I supposed Eddie Marsh would notice whether it had been pressed recently . . . or maybe Lennen had an iron at home.

I was playing tag with that sort of thing when the phone rang. It scared me. I didn't much like the idea of being asked, right then, why I'd been fooling around with fresh corpses and conspiring to suppress evidence. I let it ring three or four times, then answered.

Silence. After I'd yapped a few silly hellos, a woman's voice said, "I'm down at the corner, Doc. Can I come up?"

"Who is this?"

"I think you'll know me. Is anybody with you?"

"No. What is it you want?"

"I've got something to tell you. It's important."

I told her okay . . . to come up. On a hunch I grabbed the phone book and looked up Terry Hale. She had a listing and I called.

A man answered. "She's out. Who wants her?" He sounded as if he wasn't very happy about the whole thing. He also sounded very tough. And did I hang up? Not Old Doc Connor's strapping lad. I took a deep breath and plunged.

"This is Lieutenant Marsh's office at Police Headquarters. We want to ask her some questions."

The man laughed in a particularly nasty way and said, "Now isn't that nice. Maybe you'd like to talk to your boss. He's right here."

That was when I hung up. The distaste I developed for that receiver was sudden and overwhelming.

I didn't know much about tracing calls, and didn't think that one could be traced, but I had a nasty hunch that I'd be hearing from Eddie again any time now. Sometimes it takes me a little longer than usual to find the completely wrong way to do something, but if you leave me alone long enough I'll make it.

My mysterious visitor buzzed and I let her in. It was Terry Hale, of course. She was scared and had been crying . . . looked pretty bedraggled. Terry's a good-looking girl, maybe twenty-six or seven, with brown hair, nice eyes and respectable looking clothes . . . or does that sound too much like a man? Anyway, she looked all right to me and she definitely didn't look show-business-on-the-street. She looked like some friend's sister, maybe.

Clinically, she looked as tired as any girl of normal health would look after dancing out sixteen dollars in dimes and tips the night before. There are easier ways to make a living.

Terry didn't say anything for a minute . . . took her coat off and threw a small hat of some sort on the couch.

"Sit down."

"Thanks." She did . . . rather nicely.

"Drink? You look as though you might be able to use one."

"I guess I could at that. Yes. Thank you."

Her whiskey and soda, with mine, took a little time to fix and she got more relaxed. I sat opposite her and opened the show . . . "You're Terry Hale, aren't you?"

"Yes . . . around here." She took a careful, polite swallow from her drink . . . then a healthy one. "My right name is Gladys Eckman. You might know my father. He's a horse trainer."

"Oh? Yes, sure. I know Sam Eckman. I heard the other day that he's in town."

"He is . . . brought some horses here from Chicago. They're stabled at Empire City." The girl hesitated, sighed. "That's one of the things that make it so tough, Doc. If he wasn't here I wouldn't be in so bad a spot."

I looked at Terry Hale a long time trying to make out what she meant . . . how her father could make being a murder suspect any tougher for her.

"The trouble is about Harry Lennen, isn't it?"

"Yes." Then, "How did you know?"

"I'd seen you around with him some. That's all."

"Oh." She hesitated. "You were good to him."

"Nothing much. I looked him over once. He was coughing and losing weight. He thought he might have T.B." I lit a cigarette for her. "He didn't, though."

"I remember. Harry quit smoking for a while and got over it. You paid for his X-rays."

"I'd forgotten. Perhaps I did."

"He was broke. He was always broke."

"What sort of a fellow was he, Terry?"

"Not much, Doc. Not as right guys go, anyway. But then I don't get a chance to know too many right ones in my business. Harry and I had some things in common. Mostly bad luck. We spent a lot of our time picking each other up."

We weren't getting anyplace so I asked her what I could do for her.

She took a long drag and talked the smoke out of her lungs. "I don't know, Doc. Maybe nothing." I kept wondering how she'd act in a rage . . . with a milk bottle in her hand. She went on, "Maybe nothing. The police are questioning me. They've had me downtown twice. Now they've got a man outside my apartment."

I said, "Inside your apartment, Terry." There was no use kidding her. "Two men. One of them's Eddie Marsh. I called the place on a hunch."

"Did they know it was you calling?"

"No." Strictly with the fingers crossed.

"That helps." For the first time she looked a little lost. Her fingers snapped and unsnapped the clasp of her bag. "There's nothing there for them to find, anyway."

I couldn't see her bashing her lover over the head for ten grand . . . or for any other reason. The girl had a lot of poise and a good hold on herself.

"How badly are you involved in this thing, Terry?" She looked up as though I were making sense for the first time.

"Frankly, I don't know, Doc. There's been something going on that I didn't understand and I felt that it might be something . . . well, maybe the sort of thing I might not *want* to understand."

"Something going on where? With Harry?"

"Yes. For the last several weeks Harry's been acting queer. Nothing you could get hold of, just not himself . . . like he was afraid of something and had it on his mind all the time."

"You didn't know any reason he might have had to be afraid?"

"No . . . not if you mean enemies or danger of that sort. He told me he was going to get hold of some money . . . maybe quite a lot of it."

"When did he tell you this?" So Lennen had admitted that to her.

"About three weeks or a month ago. Then I didn't see him for some little time. I thought he might have gotten flush and brushed me off. Not long ago, one of the girls at the Parisian Gardens . . . that's where I work . . . said she saw Harry in Lindy's one night.

"He was with some other men and he was all dressed up, she told me, acting big-shot and prosperous. He owed me some money and I got sore and wrote him about it. The cops found the letter and they've been after me ever since."

She'd left too much unsaid so I asked her what was wrong with that? Why should she worry because the guy happened to owe her some dough? She squirmed a little, much more gracefully, however, than Jocko Burns had in the same spot.

"I wouldn't be worried if that were all of it. There's more. A lot more . . . although it doesn't add up to anything."

"What, for instance."

"Harry called me the night he was killed."

We were getting somewhere at last. "That adds up to something, Terry. What time did he call?"

"Very close to eight-thirty. I've thought of it since. It was my night to work late and I was getting dressed to go."

Eight-thirty. I'd have to locate Lennen at eight-thirty that night. "Did he say where he was when he called?"

"No. I'm quite sure he wasn't at home . . . there's a pay phone on the first floor there. He wasn't calling from that, I know."

"How?"

"Well, frankly, I was jealous and listened as hard as I could to figure out what he was doing. We'd been through some pretty rough times together, helping each other along . . . nickel and dime stuff, but important to us . . . then, when he got flush all of a sudden and I didn't hear from him . . . I guess you know how it would be."

"Sure. I know." It wasn't hard to see, at that. "So what made you think he wasn't home?"

"I could hear some sort of music playing. Like a band or maybe a juke-box. There were men around, too; talking loud."

"Did you hear any words?"

"It was mostly a jumble of talk. One of the men shouted something like 'Pinky on five!' There might have been other words but I don't remember."

"'Pinky on five.'"

"That was all. Just 'Pinky on five!'"

"What did Harry want?"

"He asked me to meet him at his apartment before I went to work. He knew my schedule most of the time." Terry's voice was restrained, over-quiet. I wondered whether it was caution or simply the dullness of exhaustion. I prompted her.

"So he wanted you to meet him at his place?"

"Yes."

"Right away? Then?"

"Yes. He knew I was due at work at nine." It probably was exhaustion. She didn't seem interested in what she was saying. "He said to hurry up there as soon as I could."

"Did you, Terry?"

"He said it was very important and that he . . . well, loved me and that he could explain a lot of things . . ."

"I see. And you went up?"

"Yes, Doc."

"Did you see him?"

"Not alive."

"I'm sorry, kid."

"It's okay."

"When you got there he was dead . . . there on the floor with the lights burning?"

"Yes. He was . . ." I'd have sworn her groping was genuine. ". . . he was like the papers said this morning."

". . . and how about the lights?"

"Why . . . the door was partly open . . . the lights were on. I saw the light through the door. I spoke to him and went in without knocking." She shuddered and looked awfully rocky. "I spoke to him and . . ."

"Hold it, Terry. You can't afford to do that now. It's too late to do anything but take care of yourself. You may have to do a lot of that before you get through."

"I know, Doc." I found myself waiting for her to take a big drink. She didn't. Funny how little things tell you so much about people. She just shook it off and looked up for more. "Now what?"

"How long did you stay there? Did you look around?"

"How long *did* I stay? I have no idea. Not long. I was pretty shocked, you know."

"Of course. Maybe you can figure the time. What did you do after you left?"

"I went to work. Yes. That would give you an idea of the time. It must have been around ten minutes or so after nine when I was there. I know because I got to work at twenty after . . . twenty minutes late."

There you have it. Your lover gets murdered, you stumble on his dead body, see him with his head bashed in . . . and you're twenty minutes late for your job of cheering up lonely sailors! Why? I don't know. It's just the way people do things around this circuit. It's something this town does to you. I don't mean that you get hard-boiled about things . . . it's just that you take a lot of things for granted here that would floor you anyplace else.

"Did you touch anything while you were there?"

"I don't think so. You mean fingerprints, of course."

"Yes, and anything you might have disturbed."

"I see. No, I didn't touch anything . . . anything inside, that is. I didn't think about the doorknob."

"Don't worry about that."

"Why not?"

"Doorknobs get . . . smudged pretty easily. Anyway, your print on the doorknob wouldn't mean much since you went around with Harry a lot. I doubt if there's one on it, though."

She let it go at that. Lord knows that doorknob had been polished enough!

"Do the police know you were there, Terry?"

"Not yet . . . as far as I know. They haven't said anything about it. That's one of the reasons I came here. Should I tell them about it?"

"I don't know. Offhand, I'd say yes. If you've got any reason for *not* telling them, I'd like to hear it."

"Why?"

I found myself floundering, of course. This Hale girl is smart. Yeah. That's right. Why? Am I the cops or something that I should ask what amounts to a confession from her? But I am male and had to bully my way out.

"Look here, Terry. I'm taking it for granted that you didn't kill Harry Lennen. Is that right?"

"That's right. I didn't."

"All right. You came to me for help. I don't want to advise you wrongly. If there is any reason why you don't want to tell the police everything you know . . . and you want anything further from me . . . tell me about it. If not, we'll forget the whole thing."

"Okay, Doc, okay." She crossed her handsome legs in an easy, swinging gesture that had co-ordination and strength written all over it. This girl could have swung that milk bottle in a rage. She *could* have, but I couldn't convince myself she had. Terry examined her cigarette for a while, a puzzled frown around her eyes, before she spoke. Then it came out.

"Listen, Doc." She hung those brown eyes on me without guile. "I've heard a lot of swell things about you in the last year. From Harry and from . . . different people around. They say you're a right guy . . . that you see things go on and still manage to mind your own business. They tell me you aren't too critical of us . . . our side, I mean . . . because we have to hustle a living the best way we can. It's important to me to know whether that's true."

Hello! What a gal this is! She's right, of course. I hadn't any business to cross-examine her in Jocko Burns' defense . . .

and my own. The ball was in my court and I had to come up
with an answer if I was to be half way honest about the whole
thing. At that, I had kept a lot of things to myself around the
neighborhood. Not anything very bad or even very important .
. . just the local gossip. The sporting crowd is pretty much like
a lot of old women anyway . . . I mean about little tidbits of
scandal concerning each other. Murder, of course, is something
else again.

"I think I'm an honest guy, Terry. I've tried to be. I see a lot
of cheap chiseling and stuff around that I don't like but that sort
of thing is a by-product, I'm sorry to say, of the things I like
best . . . racing, boxing, theatre. My friends aren't that kind."

"I know. You've got a lot of friends . . ." she looked up with
a little smile, "including Eddie Marsh."

"I see what you mean. Yes. I'm a good friend of Eddie's in a
way. In a lot of ways. He doesn't approve very highly of me as
a citizen, but he's a wonderful guy in his cramped style and I
respect him. But that doesn't mean that I tell him a lot of things
that aren't any of my business . . . even if they are his."

"That's what I wanted to know. I told you it's important to
me, and it is. You see, there's something else."

"Oh?"

"Yes. I'm afraid I was seen that night."

"That's not so good."

"It's worse than you know."

"Tell me about it."

"As I walked toward the apartment building, somebody
walked away from the shadows near it . . . I could see him
clearly as he came into the light."

"Had he come out of the building?"

"No. Not then, at least. But he'd been right by it . . . maybe
in the alley. I couldn't tell."

"Did he stop or turn around . . . seem to notice you?"

"No. Once he'd started, he kept on going."

"But you think he saw you."

"I'm sure he must have . . . unless he was too busy thinking
of something else at the time."

"If he came from Harry Lennen's place he had plenty to think about." There went our murderer if Terry was telling the truth. "Can you describe him? Did you get a good look at him?"

"Yes, I got a good look at him. Look, Doc, there's no use stalling around any more. It was my father."

"Sam Eckman!"

"Yes. You see why I couldn't figure out what to say to the police."

I poured her another drink. I had to think about things.

"Yes. That makes it different."

"Very."

"If he was close enough for you to recognize him, he must have recognized you."

"Maybe not. I was dressed for work . . . evening wrap and a furpiece around my neck. He hasn't seen me much lately, especially dressed like ten thousand women in that section at that hour."

"Could be. He didn't see you enter the building?"

"No."

"You waited?"

"I didn't have to. He never looked back. I turned directly into the entrance so he wouldn't see me if he did."

So it was Sam Eckman. Could be at that. Terry's statement about Sam pretty well cleared her in my mind, too . . . or it seemed to. She'd hardly implicate her father when she needn't have said anything about it at all. On the other hand, suppose her father had seen her *coming out* of Harry's instead of approaching as she had said?

Yes, it might have been Eckman. Then it would be horses. Then it would be very dirty. There isn't much nastiness on the race track despite what leering friends tell you they know. Racing, like baseball, is strictly big business these days and its life . . . political and popular alike . . . depends on its legitimacy. The real policemen of horse racing are not the uniformed Pinkerton men you see at the track, but a comparatively small group of gray old gentlemen who are the stewards, judges and secretaries . . . carrying out the edicts of that even smaller group of gray old gentlemen who tread the hallowed precincts of the Jockey Club.

These gentlemen love racing for itself, carrying on staunchly in the belief that horse races are held because one man thinks his horse can run faster and farther than the other fellow's. With people who attempt to run races for less sporting reasons, they are likely to take quick, violent and permanent measures.

But occasionally some trainer, or even a minor official, decides to commit professional suicide for money. You don't get three strikes in that league. One offense and you're back in the livery stable business. One offense and you're stopped at the gate of any track in America. The Pinks know a thousand faces.

As a result, when somebody does sell his racing birthright for a mess of thousand dollar bills, it's usually a pretty dirty affair . . . and as large a deal as he can make it.

Terry was walking around looking at diplomas . . . or through them. "Listen, Terry." She swung around, startled. I guess we hadn't said anything for quite a while.

"Yes, Doc?"

"Did your father know Harry Lennen?"

"He . . ." Her voice made me look up quickly at her. I had a sudden hunch she was about to lie to me. Maybe not. I just felt that way. "He might have. I didn't know much about my father's business . . . or his friends."

"Did Lennen ever mention your father? Talk about him?"

"I . . . can't remember that he did . . ." There wasn't any use in pushing the girl into further lies . . . or evasions . . . or whatever these phony statements were. I felt certain the rest of her story had been straight and I decided to get her back to that basis again.

"Okay, Terry, I just had a notion that there must have been some connection between them . . . and that it's pretty likely to have something to do with Harry's death."

"I suppose so. I'd hate to think it was that way. You say you know my father . . ."

Sure I knew Sam. I'd seen him around a lot . . . a strictly small-time, shed-row operator with eight or ten cheap horses, shrewd in the ways of racing, contributing little to the sport and taking what he could. There are lots of them around. Good horsemen, always, making their living from purse-money, as a rule . . . seldom from bets.

". . . and nobody who knows him could possibly imagine him mixed up with anything as . . . as terrible as this."

The old-timers always said Sam was honest.

". . . He's so easy-going and friendly. He's got a bad temper and flies off once in a while but not . . . what would you call it? Vicious. As long as I can remember he's just loved the races and never cared if he had a dime as long as he could be around the track."

"You said you suspected something was going on with Lennen. Did you sense that around your father, too?"

"I didn't see much of him, Doc. We've never had too much in common and our working hours . . . well, I'm checking out about the time he's getting his breakfast. Within a couple of hours. No. I've never gotten that impression from him in the three or four times I've seen him since he got here from the West."

"Has he got any money?" There was always that ten grand to be considered.

"Not to speak of. When my mother died and I came to New York, he rented our house in Chicago. He has that. I guess he doesn't do too badly with the horses."

"I hear he gets along. Doesn't bet much."

"He never did. I can remember him saying 'a man's sucker enough to *own* the damn things, leave alone *bet* on them.' That's like him."

"Makes sense, too." I got up and finished my drink. "What do you want me to do?"

"I don't know exactly. The cops in my room make it worse than I thought. I suppose they might even pick me up. I wish you could figure this thing out some way. I can't believe my father had anything to do with Harry's . . . death . . . but I'm so afraid I might say something or . . . You see I don't *know* anything!"

I turned her around by the shoulders. "Don't you, Terry?"

Johnstown, as a three-year-old, could have run a furlong before she spoke. Then she looked up and said, "No, Doc, I don't know anything that could possibly account for . . . what happened."

I herded her toward the door. As casually as I could, I said, "By the way. It just occurred to me that you might have gone back to the apartment later that night for some reason. Did you?"

Terry Hale looked up at me with a very serious face, but I had the annoying feeling that her big eyes were laughing at me. She looked like she was about to wink.

"Oh, no! Of course not. Why would you ask?"

"I've got a hunch that somebody will ask you that and you'd better be ready to prove that you didn't."

"I've already told you I was back at work at nine-twenty."

"Sure. I know." The place she worked was a madhouse most evenings . . . noise, crowds and confusion. It would be rough to keep track of anybody. Oh well. "Yes. That's right. You told me."

She was still laughing with those eyes. I didn't like it. At that, though, I hadn't caught her looking for the bump on my head.

As I let her out I got over my pique long enough to make a small speech . . . "Well, kid, it won't do either of us any good if you're seen here. Go home and face the cops again. Eddie Marsh is a fair guy and if you and your father weren't mixed up too badly in this, you've got nothing to be scared about."

She started down the stairs instead of using the elevator. I called after her. "In the meantime, I'll do anything I can to help."

"Thanks, Doc. They always told me you were . . . one of the best."

A good kid. A good kid and no killer or I'm the biggest chump on Broadway.

Well, maybe. I heard the door slam and the phone ring at the same time.

It was Katie.

5

N.B.C. was a hive of something or other as I waited at the Forty-
ninth Street door for Katie. To meet her at that entrance was a
good sign, by the way. Whenever Katie took one of her infrequent notions to slum my end of town she asked me to meet
her in Forty-ninth. Most of the time, when she was her lofty
self and wished to be escorted thither . . . where *people* live . . .
it was Fiftieth. We get one-way-streetish, hereabouts, not only
in our movements but in our thinking. To me, a visit to Katie's
place was a Sunday-suit excursion into respectability. To Katie,
a trip to my neighborhood was not only publicly but personally
iniquitous.

To some amazing number of radio listeners, unwillingly
classified as housewives, Katie is Miss Storm . . . Homemaker.
Miss Storm I'll have you know, M.A., Col. '45! But don't let
that throw you. Katie's a showman. She can handle a gag or sing
a ballad with the best. She does, too, which accounts for *Recipes
in Rhythm, There's a Kick in the Kitchen* and the fact that half
the big names in show business will guest on Katie's show for
free . . . strictly for laughs.

It is unfortunate, but honorable, I suppose, to note here
that Miss Storm makes more money than I ever saw . . . Uncle
Will and all. Her pay-check would buy her the full-time of a
more eminent medical man than I . . . if she had any use for
either of us. She's healthy as a halfback, which bars the other
guy, and she's sane, which lets me out.

On the other hand, Katie is very beautiful, which lines up a flock of other guys at her door, to whom she pays no attention, and she's a social-worker at heart, which keeps her interested in me. In the absence of any motive more flattering, I'll take that. I'm not proud.

So I waited at N.B.C., happy as a flea with a whole dog to himself. Over the phone, the queen of love and beauty had said to be sure to meet her tonight. I noted that wash-your-hands-before-dinner-company's-coming tone which gives me encouragement at rare intervals.

The usual cabs stopped and let the usual people out and carried the other usual people away. Occasionally there would be someone in makeup. Television probably. Or coming from the theatre for a guest shot. I thought of the original script of *One Touch of Venus* which I had read for a friend. They had two identical Abraham Lincolns meeting in the revolving doors of N.B.C. I never quite forgave them for deleting it.

Katie erupted from the doorway. "Hi, Doc!" She was fresh from rehearsal for tomorrow's show. *Fresh* from rehearsal and no kidding if you know the Storm child. She loves radio business. She *is* radio business! "Hello, darling."

"I'm hungry, Doc, and I want to talk."

"Wonderful! We'll eat and talk. I've got a lot of things to report, too." All jolly and up-tempo, I thought it sounded, but with Katie you get away with nothing.

"Oh, oh. You look sheepish. Have you broken a window?"

"Sort of."

"What've you been up to?"

"Murder and stuff. I'll tell you about it. Where'll we go?"

"I've been thinking about the Lafayette lately."

"Right. Let's grab a cab." I whistled. I'll whistle for you sometime. I can stop a cab at two hundred yards. It fascinates Katie.

The trip to Ninth and University Place was pretty much occupied with ritualistic things we always did in taxicabs . . . some pleasant squirming about getting settled, the lighting of cigarettes, a certain interlocking of elbows, patting of hands and such exclamations as "Well!" and "Gosh, I'm glad to see you!" Nothing much else.

At the Lafayette, Albert greeted us, bowing deeply from the management. We chose the café in preference to the larger dining room for reasons not pertinent to the plot and followed François' large Gallic grin to our favorite table.

Through two pairs of martinis, we dodged the subject of broken windows. The veal à la Holstein and head lettuce with Roquefort dressing provided their own topic for a time, then . . .

"Can we get to your sins now?" Katie sat there, heart-breakingly beautiful, making me think of a lot of things besides my game of cops-'n'-robbers. "Frankly, I had somewhat better opinion of you than murder. Did you commit it?"

"That, my angel, is still unsolved. I haven't the remotest idea who'll turn up in the last chapter. It might as well be me as anybody."

"Make it quick. I'm getting fussy and the dinner was too good to indigest. What is it and how did you get mixed up in it?" Katie took a cigarette, settled back and I knew I was on.

"Well, it was this way . . ." I went through it all . . . Jocko's visit, my ill-advised corpse-stalking, Eddie Marsh, Terry Hale and the rest. I could fairly hear Katie's alert mind ticking, snapping up facts, filing and cross filing them for reference, whipping in an occasional question—which never failed to connect. Finally she grinned. Katie Storm has the sweetest smile in the world . . . a grown-up, understanding offering that would make any guy happy. But when she grins like an urchin, I'm a dead pigeon.

"So you haven't had that second call from Lieutenant Marsh yet."

"No. And I'm scared as hell to go home."

"You are?"

"You aren't just kidding. I was a chump to get into the thing in the first place; now it's snowballing on me. Marsh will have my hide for holding out what I know already . . . leave alone what more I've got to learn before I dare to talk to him again. I'm plenty scared to go home."

Katie grinned again. I suppose I had the bad grace to pout this time. At any rate I was floundering around in my problems. Whatever it was, it must have been effective because Katie leaned across the table and put her hand on mine.

"Don't cry, little man, it's nothing but a murder-mystery. I'll go home with you and hold your hand."

I had a blinding attack of acute euphoria.

"You'll what?"

"I said, as simply and as distinctly as my food permits, that I'd go home with you."

"That's what I thought you said."

"I believe I added that I'd hold your hand because you are frightened of your telephone, and of certain repercussions from your broken window. I don't believe I said anything more than that. Did I?"

"No."

"Then why are you leering at me?"

"Was I leering at you?"

"You *are* leering at me." Katie took her hand off mine. "You might as well stand by to unleer, too, because when you look like that, you don't need anybody to hold your hand."

"When I leer?"

"When you look broadway and . . . wise-guy . . . and . . . un-you!"

"Then why do you kid about things like that? You know perfectly well that I can't . . . ."

"Kid about things like that! Have you ever heard me *say* anything like that before? Why would I be kidding? Oh, Jimmy! You're such a damned fool about things. Don't you understand? If you're going to play murder games over in that slum section of yours, I'm sitting in! And besides . . . ."

"Besides what?"

"Porglescrob!" said Katie.

I knew from long and bitter experience that such a Katian oath put an end to any subject and I didn't pursue it. I'd have liked to, though, because it was about to be one of Katie's infrequent sentimentalities.

As a peace offering, I blew her to cognac. Real. In snifters. I wish someone would tell me why snifters sometime. It was fun and, after lolling around in the brandy for a while, I felt pretty well up to facing my phone.

We hailed a hack and ground our way back uptown. Katie showed unusual concern for my welfare. She held onto my hand and the two kisses which she rationed out to me on the way home were a little on the maternal side. They're nice too. I think maybe I should take up some permanently hazardous occupation like nightwatchman.

As we pulled up I half expected to see a cop at the apartment door but all was serene. Katie made her customary tour of inspection to see whether my housekeeping was up to its ordinary slovenly standards. I made a pitcher of ice water and opened fresh cigarettes while she decided I hadn't gone native and we settled down to mull over the murder. The telephone sat on the little table between us and looked expectant.

"Look, Doc. Somebody has to have seen Lennen alive sometime or other. Everyone, so far, has been stumbling over his corpse." She wrinkled up her nose and gave me one of those quick, professional glances with which alert women keep track of their personal progress in even the most serious conversation. It annoys Katie to be reminded of it. I should learn not to.

She caught me checking up on her. "Peeking again, aren't you!" She did what I suppose writers mean when they say somebody snorted.

"I peeking? *You* were peeking. You were giving me the how-am-I-doing department."

"I was giving you nothing of the kind. I know perfectly well how I'm doing."

"Ouch!"

"I was making a penetrating and worthwhile observation about your murder. Somebody, I was saying, has to have seen Harry Lennen alive in that apartment. Who was it?"

"As very often happens in sudden killings like this one, I suspect that the last person to see him alive was the murderer."

"Don't get smart. Two people say they saw him dead. One other person, Eckman, had probably been at the apartment. Then the person who hit you . . . who's either one of them or somebody new. There's your list."

I added them up . . . Burns, Terry Hale, Sam Eckman and whoever bopped me. Katie went on . . .

"Of course the last person we *know* saw Lennen alive . . . say within forty minutes of his death . . . *could* have seen him both alive and dead."

"From that delightful bit of Stoopnaglia I judge you mean the mysterious 'Pinky on five?'"

Katie nodded thoughtfully. "Have you been able to make any sense out of that?"

I'd forgotten "Pinky on five," or at least I hadn't puzzled over it much. It was one of the things I couldn't tell Eddie Marsh and his tough cops. "It could mean anything. It could mean a rare hamburger on the number five lunch."

"It could mean a bowling alley . . . pin-boy Pinky was supposed to go to work on alley number five." She grinned. "Or is that too silly?"

"Silly? The whole damned thing is silly, so far. It could have been an enthusiastic papa playing games with his infant's itty-bitty-pinkies."

"That *is* silly. Terry Hale said the man shouted."

"I said an 'enthusiastic' papa, didn't I? You've no idea how loud I'd shout if . . ."

"Lieutenant Marsh hasn't any sense of humor, my friend, and, for the moment, I haven't either."

"So I see."

"Even the possibility of propagating the Forty-eighth Street Jukes makes me shudder. I think I'll have a drink . . . don't get up. I feel like moving around." She dumped a cigarette and started wandering about the room.

I lay on the back of my neck and contemplated my sins. Pinky on five seemed a world away. I was dabbling with eminence again when Katie turned from my precious print of War Admiral and Seabiscuit leaving the gate at Pimlico. Clem McCarthy gave it to me.

"You know, Jimmy?"

"What?"

"If I'd been in my office and someone had shouted 'Katie on two,' I'd have answered the telephone."

I got off my neck and hollered "Hey!"

"Makes sense, doesn't it? We have two lines."

"Sure it makes sense! That's it. Good shot, darling . . . it couldn't be anything else."

"Someplace with five lines."

"Right. Five or more." There they were, all the elements of our little drama . . . a tout and bookmaker, a horse trainer, his daughter, the victim, a hanger-on with gamblers and Pinky on five. Five telephone lines made it a bookie-joint and Pinky a bookmaker or sheetwriter. I didn't know any bookmaker called Pinky, or even one with red hair. I told Katie so. She went out into the kitchen and rattled around with ice-trays and glasses.

Terry Hale had said she was called at eight-thirty or close to that. I wondered if the fact that Pinky had been called on line five meant that the other four were busy . . . or that there was an operator on duty. It didn't put together when you considered the hour. What would a bookmaker's office be so busy that late for? Katie came back with the drinks and I put it up to her. She was practical about it as usual and dialed a number on the telephone.

"This is Katie Storm. Is Nippy on? . . . Thanks." She put her hand over the transmitter. "This gal will know. She knows everything about telephones." Then, "Hi, Nip, Katie Storm. Tell me . . . on some sort of private telephone, when somebody says 'Jones on five' what does it mean? . . . I don't know what kind nor where . . . yes . . . would they have an operator on that sort of a set-up? . . . I see . . . ." This went on for some time. Finally Katie hung up.

I said, "I judge that was Nippy."

"It was, and I know all about it. She runs the professional women's answering service. Now. It could have been a theater ticket agency."

"Yeah?"

"Yeah. Or a whole lot of other things. With as many as five lines . . . trunks, Nip said . . . the chances are against its being a private office. The man shouting for 'Pinky on five' makes it pretty certain that there wasn't an operator on duty . . . but could be."

"Then who figures out which line is which then?"

"The telephone company. No. Machines do it. The phone company's machines."

"Come now. You pick up a phone and dial a number . . ."

"Right. You pick up a phone and dial a number . . . Circle 9-4700."

"Yeah, yeah."

"Don't say 'yeah, yeah' like that. You don't know a damned thing about it and besides, you sound like you were trying to sound like a character. Listen."

"I did listen."

"All right. You call Circle 9-4700. That number has five trunks . . . outside lines. Actually they are Circle 9-4701, 2, 3 and so forth, but you don't know it."

"Why don't I?"

"Because you don't have to. The phone company's got an automatic toggleplop which passes up the busy lines and flips into the first open one . . . in this case, line five."

"Then those lines were busy. The first four."

"Probably. But if it was a switchboard where they have an operator on duty during the day, she always leaves the different lines plugged into different telephones around the place so people can make calls from their desks if they work late. See?"

"Then if the first four lines were busy, the call would come in on whatever phone wasn't?"

"Right. Unless the person outside knew enough to call that exact line . . . like Circle 9-4705. Then it would ring direct."

"All of which means we don't know any more about it than we did."

"That isn't quite true. It stands to reason that the person who called didn't know Pinky's particular line."

"Why not?"

"Because the man said 'Pinky on five.' He didn't say just 'Hey, Pinky! Telephone.' If Pinky had had one of the lines plugged into his regular desk that's what the man would have hollered."

"That makes sense. But what if Pinky was just a visitor . . . hanger-on or something?"

"Then the man would have said the same thing . . . 'Hey, Pinky! Telephone . . . over here,' or something like that."

That made sense, too. It was a fair guess that Pinky belonged there, that it was the sort of place where anybody answered the telephone nearest him and that the other four lines were busy. When I told Katie that it pretty well bore out my bookie-joint theory she tossed a casual monkey wrench.

"Wouldn't what the Hale girl said about the music knock that theory out? A juke-box or something?"

"I suppose so." Certainly no bookie in his right mind would have a juke-box around to distract his serious horse-players. Even if the place were a lay-off office . . . one of the bookmakers' clearing houses where customers never appeared . . . music would hardly be part of the picture. Besides that, what would four lines of a bookmaker's office be busy for at eight-thirty in the evening? There seemed to be nothing to do but find Pinky. He, or somebody with him there that night, was one of the last people to have anything to do with Harry Lennen. "My guess is that Pinky, or somebody he knows, could answer a lot of questions for us."

"Then we find Pinky?"

"Then *I* find Pinky. I suspect he won't be too anxious to be found . . . especially to be identified with Lennen. There's no Baedecker for this end of town and I don't relish some of the places I'll have to go looking for him. If he is a bookmaker and is tangled up in this thing, I don't want you in on it."

"Maybe you're right." Katie reached for her hat and gloves . . . both gloves, not like the song. "When you need some detecting over in my end of town give me a call." She went to the mirror. "I've got to go."

"I knew I shouldn't have mentioned the neighborhood."

"That's right." Katie rubbed up The Nose.

"I'll let you know when I catch up with Pinky."

"Mmmmmm." Lipsticking going on.

While she was looking over the paint job I put her coat around her shoulders. "Have a nice time, darling?"

"Very. Thank you." She dropped the tools in a pocket and wrangled her arms into the sleeves.

"Will you come again . . . soon?"

"Of course I will." Katie faced me. "Jimmy . . ."

"What?"

"You'll be careful . . . I mean about this whole business . . . Pinky and all?" You could have heard me purr down at the corner.

"Of course I'll be careful. You have to be careful when you nose into this sort of thing. These guys don't kid around. Once they get into something like this, they go all the way. A murder rap . . ."

"Look, Jimmy . . ." I knew I was in for it, but I got a grin and a hug for the beating. "Look, Jimmy, you don't have to read the script for me, you big ham. Just be careful and don't get into too much trouble . . . will you?"

I spent the next five minutes proving that I had everything to live for.

"O.K., darling, I'll take you home."

"You'll wait right here for your police call. Besides, I wouldn't trust you in a cab in your present condition. You'd probably get lost on the way back and wind up in saloons."

So we rattled down in the little elevator and up to Seventh Avenue for a taxicab. I watched the taillight lose itself in the traffic and felt pretty lonely as I wandered back. I started digging for my keys and remembered I'd left the apartment door open.

Eddie Marsh was sitting on the couch.

6

Eddie got up as I came in.

"Hello, Doc. I saw you putting Katie Storm into a cab so I came on up. Okay?"

"Sure, Eddie. Glad to see you. Sit down and have a drink."

"Thanks, I will. I'm all through for the night." Eddie sat down again and settled himself like he intended to be there a while. He's a big guy, light-heavyweight in size, and good-looking in a noble sort of way. Fit, too. I've boxed with him at a gym we make together a couple of times a week and he's good.

The drink gave me a minute to decide what I could tell him and what I wanted him to tell me. If I was that lucky. I couldn't figure it out and gave it up. I'd just have to take it as it came and stay out of all the trouble I could. I could count on the big fellow's friendship to a point where it began to interfere with his business. No further.

He settled back with his glass and grinned his appreciation. "Got half an hour?"

I told him I had.

"I'm trying to check up on the Lennen killing, Doc, and I've got a feeling you can be helpful . . . maybe I should say more helpful."

Oh, oh. "Why sure, Eddie, I'll help all I can."

Marsh looked up from a careful study of his brogans. "Will you?"

Oh brother! I wished I didn't know the guy so well. He was neatly setting me up for a left hook and I wasn't going to be

49

able to block it. If I'd only known what he'd got hold of. Terry Hale? Had Jocko been tied up with it and brought in? Either of them could have left me in a spot where I'd have a bad half hour with Eddie. I'd stall as long as I could . . . "Of course I've already told you that I didn't ever have much to do with Lennen."

"Yes." He resumed his survey of the extended feet. "Of course. That goes for the people around Lennen, too, I suppose. Or does it?"

I was floundering around and looking for some sort of a hole when the cop laughed a little and said, "Look, Doc. I'm not going to dig around trying to find out what you know or what you don't know. I have no idea why you are getting so cagey about the thing and, for the moment, I'm taking it for granted you know what you're doing."

Good old Eddie. I took my first comfortable breath but said nothing. How I said nothing!

"You see, Doc, there are a lot of things I don't know and would like to find out. I have reason to believe you know at least some of them."

There still wasn't anything for me to say so I buried my face in my drink. He didn't seem to expect an answer anyway.

"In most homicide cases, the Department knows who the corpse was and they scour around like a lot of bird dogs because they don't know who the murderer is. In this one, we are pretty certain who the killer is and we're losing our minds trying to find out who got killed."

Hold everything! So they've got somebody to arrest already but can't figure out the connection between the killer and Lennen. I said I didn't get it.

"It's simple enough. Harry Lennen wasn't Harry Lennen. As nearly as we can make out, he's been Harry Lennen for about two years."

". . . and before that?"

Marsh spread out his hands. "Blank. He wasn't anybody."

"Fingerprints?"

"Plenty, of course. All over the rooms and all in their proper places on the corpse. They just don't mean anything. No criminal record, no draft board or service record . . . no nothing. The man simply doesn't . . . didn't . . . exist."

"These people you mentioned, Eddie . . . these people around him. Don't they know anything about him?"

He laughed to take the sting out of it and said, "What people do you mean, Doc?" He waited long enough to pick up his drink and added, "No they don't know . . . or at least claim they don't know . . . anything before he turned up here."

"You think the motive for the killing comes from farther back than that, then."

"We do. We've traced the guy's activities since he became Harry Lennen. Thoroughly, too. As far as the murder itself is concerned, anything could have led to it. Somebody got sore and sapped him with a milk bottle . . . anybody could have done it . . . anybody who could swing the bottle and could get mad enough. But there's one thing that's out of key with all of that."

"The money, of course."

"Right." Marsh made a huge pyramid of his homely shoes by balancing the heel of one on the toe of the other. He looked a little startled at the towering display and pulled both feet back under him. "You see, the ten grand makes it something else again. Harry Lennen, at least the one we know, didn't have any ten thousand dollar friends. He didn't have anything about his whole existence which was that big. Nobody'd give him that much for any services he could conceivably render. Nobody with any sense would have lent him that much and certainly nobody would have trusted him with ten grand as far as he could see him."

"Lord, no." Harry was strictly a nickel-and-dime guy. "What about his having stolen it?"

"No. That's just as off-key. Lennen didn't think in that kind of numbers . . . let alone operate in them. If the dough had been stolen from a legitimate source, we'd have heard about it. If it hadn't and those guys went to get it back, they'd have damned well got it back and not left it on him."

"Looks like he wasn't killed for the ten grand at all. Or, if he was killed *on account* of the money, the guy didn't know he had it."

"That's the way I figure it. But there's nothing we can dig up about him as Harry Lennen that could hook him up with both the money *and* . . . whoever killed him."

"Who did kill him, Eddie? You said you were pretty certain."

He looked pleased as hell with himself as if he'd been afraid I wouldn't ask him. "I'm not sure I'd tell you anyway, Doc, but it's a cinch I'm not going to while you're still holding out on me."

"What do you mean . . . holding out?" By that time I was hoping he'd tell me. At least I'd find out what he thought I knew.

"Look. You're a good friend of mine and have been ever since you got out of uniform. I like you. I don't care much for your chosen career of loiterer and, as a cop, I'm a professional enemy of half the people you loiter with. But I've got a hell of a lot of respect for your honesty and your loyalty . . . to *all* your friends, on or off the police force."

"Thanks, Eddie." I don't suppose I looked as guilty as I felt.

"That's why I haven't wanted to press the matter as long as I had any other way of getting the information I need. For the time being, tell me what you feel like telling, Doc. As much as you can. You know, of course, that if we need the rest badly enough, we'll get it. Right now, I'd hate like hell to embarrass you and . . . well . . . it looks from here like I might have to."

The business of my sitting there and looking innocent was wearing pretty thin. I couldn't get anyplace until I learned, somehow, what he knew . . . and where he'd learned it. I'd passed the point where I could look smugly mysterious at the guy as if we were playing Twenty Questions.

"Embarrass me how, Eddie?"

"Either socially . . ." He leered as only the not-yet-worldly can leer. Is there anything more unpleasant? ". . . or with the authorities. It's this way. Harry Lennen, a low-grade bum of the sporting world, gets himself brained with a milk bottle. His girl is questioned by the police, as would be expected, then comes galloping up here to see you . . . father-confessor to the impious . . ."

"Terry Hale."

"Gladys Terry Hale Eckman." The big cop was having a lot of fun, but I didn't kid myself that his purpose was any less serious. It could get very unfunny for both of us and neither of us wanted it that way. I guess I took too long answering him because he said . . .

"You could tell me she came here for professional attention and I'd almost believe you. She certainly looked like she needed it when we were talking to her. She's got something on her mind besides what she told us and I thought you might just possibly know what it is."

"Did she tell you she came to see me?"

"Definitely not."

"Then may I ask how you knew she came?"

"Doc. Even New York City detectives sometimes detect things. We found out about your date with Hale by the simple expedient of having one of our young men follow her up the street the other night. As I remember it, he didn't even need to whip out his false whiskers. She went into the cigar store, called up, came out and pushed your button in the entrance. Half an hour later she came down. So?"

"So. She did just that."

"Incidentally, while she was visiting you, I was having a look around her place and didn't want to get caught at it. Some dope called up for her and, when she didn't answer, the guy said it was my office. At least it gave us a laugh. After I found out where she'd gone I decided the comedian had to be you."

I dreaded his next statement . . . hoped he might have overlooked the point . . . but not Eddie Marsh. "Adding up the fact that you obviously hadn't seen Terry Hale when you called and the fact that you associated her name with my office, I couldn't help wondering where you fit in. So you see, Doc, we're interested in you now. Not officially yet, because I've kept a lot of stuff to myself. But we can't overlook you very long."

"I see."

"Mind telling me what Terry Hale wanted . . . or what you wanted of her?"

"No. You had her scared and she knew I'd done a couple of small professional favors for Lennen and she wanted me to help her straighten the thing out."

"How?"

"She thought it looked bad for her because Harry owed her some money . . . I don't know how much . . ."

"Two hundred dollars."

"That's a lot of dimes to dance out. Anyway, she said some of the other girls knew Lennen was apparently giving her the brush-off and that you had found a pretty stiff letter she'd written him about it."

"That's right. We have the letter."

"I told her I'd do what I could and she has promised me to check anything I run into which she might recognize as having any connection with Lennen. If she knew anything now about his connection with gamblers or any sort of hustlers of the ten thousand dollar variety I'm sure she would have told me . . . and you."

"But she gave you a lead of some sort."

I stalled with my drink, thinking what a fool I was not to tell Eddie the whole story. Not a person in the bunch of them meant anything whatever to me . . . Burns, Hale, Eckman . . . chances were I was helping some killer cover up his tracks. Meantime I was getting into trouble.

"Tell me one thing, Doc." Eddie was serious and a little mad. "Are you under some sort of pressure in this?"

"No. I'll tell you exactly what I'm up against. It isn't anything much. I've got a tip . . . half tip and half hunch . . . that I can find out where that ten thousand bucks came from. If I tell you about it and I'm wrong, you'll have to put a man I know pretty well out of business; if I'm right, you'll have what you need to wrap up the case . . . if knowing where the money came from will do it."

"I think that's what we need." Eddie put down his glass. "Damn your gangster ethics, Doc, you'll have me walking a beat again over this thing. What do you intend to do?"

What did I intend to do . . . at least what could I do that I could tell Marsh? I made a stab at it. . . . "I want to nose around a little in a couple of spots you couldn't get in without a squad

. . . then you'd get nothing. It won't take me long. I may have to go from one person to another a little, but I can run it out, right or wrong, in a couple of days. Can you give me that?"

"I suppose so. I had hoped Terry Hale might have given you some hint as to Lennen's identity. That would go a long way toward clearing things up too. Did she . . . or is that one of the things you aren't telling me?"

"No, she didn't . . . and that's straight. As a matter of fact, she gave me the impression that Lennen didn't know too much about her and that she knew nothing at all about him. I asked her about that."

"Her father's a horse trainer. Know him?"

"Yes, in a way. I've known Sam Eckman around. He seems to be pretty much all right." I wasn't happy with any of this . . . least of all with the shift to Eckman. Two down and one to go. All Eddie had to do now, was to mention Jocko Burns and I would have blown the works. If I hadn't made my call on the corpse and had that to confess, I think I'd have told him anyway. That was too serious. I held my breath until he changed the subject.

"If it will help you any, Lennen got the ten thousand the day he was killed."

"How did you figure that?"

The guy laughed and I felt better about him. "I told you we get around to detecting once in a while. The needle and thread he used to sew the bills in his coat were on top of his bed."

"Smart."

"Why not? Anything else you got you think I should know?"

"Not now. I'll see you in a couple of days and spill it all one way or the other. If I get anything that's the slightest use to you, I'll bring it in whether it closes up this guy or not. That's a promise."

"O.K., Doc." The big fellow got up and reached for his hat. "Thanks for the drink. If anybody bops you over the head with a bottle let me know."

Then he was gone. I suppose the crack was natural enough under the circumstances, but I still didn't like it. Eddie Marsh had put his whole soul into the delivery of it.

You know, it could have been a milk bottle at that.

7

I woke, next morning, to the din of bouncing ashcans and that loud, cheerful dialogue which early workers everywhere seem to share. The bedtable clock showed five-forty-five and I marveled at the fact that I had both eyes open. Then, of course, I knew what was tugging me awake. There would be smoke curling up from the hot water tubs at Empire City, the horses would be finishing off their hay and the work of the morning would be under way. Somewhere, out there, Sam Eckman would be going about his business with things in his mind I needed to know.

I got up and threw on some clothes. There would be time enough for bathing, shaving and a decent breakfast later. Coffee at the corner helped me make the Jerome Avenue subway and a cab from the cemetery at the end of the line hauled me the rest of the way.

I rolled down the window at the gate and asked the Pinkerton where Eckman was stabled. He ambled back in his shed and consulted his list.

"Ten . . . barn ten . . . first turn left and ten barns over." Then, as the driver started up, "If one of them bums is gonna win, let me know, willyah, Doc?"

I gave him a double take because I couldn't remember him. The Pinks know everybody. I climbed out at barn ten and paid off.

Eckman's layout wasn't much different from anybody else's . . . I counted ten stalls and a feedroom beside the tackroom. Fair-sized outfit and apparently well run. You can pretty well

tell at a glance when you know something about it. A racing
barn is neat. Every halter hung precisely in the center of the
open upper door, shanks carefully rolled. Feed tubs hung outside the stalls . . . one in such a position that the trainer would
see the quantity of oats left by a horse which didn't finish his
breakfast. Tubs, buckets, sheets and coolers all in the maroon
and green of Sam's racing colors.

Four men were mucking out the stalls when I got there.
That's quite a lot of help for nine and a pony these days. One
of the ginnies looked light enough to gallop horses . . . maybe
two of them, for there was another whose weight looked hard
to guess . . . a long guy with small bone and not much meat on
him. One hundred and thirty-five is not too heavy for steady,
slow work. For the horse, I mean.

Eckman was nowhere to be seen. I braced one of the men as
he came back from the manure-pit with his mucksack. "Good
morning. Where's the boss?"

The guy looked at me for a moment and said, "He's over
at the kitchen," and went on with his work. I looked around a
while, recognizing a few of the horses. Big old hammer-headed
Dustpan, once a fair sort, but bad-legged and getting old. Still
a tough horse to beat over a distance of ground when he is
right. They were all pretty much like that, around twenty-five
to thirty-five hundred-dollar platers. That's the sort Sam had
always had and probably always would have.

One thing was sure. Unless I was missing something as I
reviewed names, recognized most, looked at fired knees and
ankles and generally sniffed around, there wasn't a horse in
the lot consistent or able enough to warrant any connection
with ten thousand dollars. That went for purchase price as well.
They just weren't that kind of horses.

One of the men went into Dustpan's stall and I stood watching him knocking the dirt off the big fellow. An old-timer, evidently, because he made that attention-distracting hissing noise
as he groomed which you get to associate with English and Irish
grooms. I said, "I've seen that fellow come out of the clouds to
win many a time."

The man didn't look up. "He can still run a little in the last part of it." He moved around the horse. "Whoa, daddy!"

That was it. I'd thought so. Top horse in the barn. They don't ordinarily call them mom and daddy unless they are. "Sam got anything new this year?" The fellow went to his tack box for something.

"A couple. That bay filly down at the other end is new. We claimed her at Arlington. There's one or two more. They're a common lot."

"Sam always does all right with that sort."

"We ain't doing bad." He went back into the stall and I moved on. Sam Eckman came along with the feed man who was apparently taking an order. I waited by the lead pony . . . a big capable looking chunk with a blazed face. Sam went through the usual routine about the lousy bedding, man couldn't get decent straw any more; stuff you've been giving us is more trouble than it's worth. Well, okay, then. See that you do!

"Good morning, Sam." He peered at me, then grinned.

"Why, hello, Doc Connor! Last time I seen you, you were on leave from someplace."

"I was just getting out, Sam. How goes it?"

"Not too bad, Doc. We been winning a few. You back practicing?"

"Not very active yet. I've been sort of loafing for a while."

"Why not? You guys earned it, I guess . . . Wait a minute, will you? . . . Curly! Put the tack on the big horse and the bay mare. That's right. They'll be the first set and work slow. I want 'em out of the way because there's two light boys due here at eight o'clock to work the colt and Cherub. We'll pony the cougher later . . ."

Eckman turned again to me. "Well, it's good to see you, Doc. I sure wished for you a month or two ago."

"How come?"

"Hell! I had four times as many sore legs in the barn as I had horses. There ain't a vet left on the racetrack that knows the first damned thing about legs any more. I never see a better man with sore horses than you."

"Thanks. That's the kind of practice I like. I wish I'd known. How they coming now?"

"Oh I got them around somehow. They're standing up fair."

"I'll bet they are. Did you ever have a sound-legged horse, Sam?" The old fellow looked at me and laughed like a man with nothing on his conscience. "Never a good one, Doc. Seems I always get 'em when they're pretty well stove up. I got no kick coming though. I couldn't afford to keep a good horse if I had one."

There are a lot of men like Sam in the racing business . . . men who have tremendous skill and patience with horses other trainers have cast off as bad risks. Old Dustpan was a perfect example. He was cut out to be a good one . . . a stake horse . . . when he went bad in the knees. Hard preparation for the juvenile stakes had taken its toll, as it always does, of the two year olds, and Dustpan's name was on the casualty list.

"Be around a while, Doc? I'm working a few this morning."

Casual. Hardly like Sam had associated me with Terry or Lennen. I wished for an instant I'd made some sort of agenda for my meeting with Sam. It could be that I'd be telling all the wrong things to the wrong guy. But again, I'd have to play it as it came.

"Not long, Sam. I'd like to stay around but I've got to get back. I wanted to see you about something."

"Yeah? Why sure, Doc. Take long?"

"Maybe a while."

"Okay. Look. Let me get these fellows under way here and I'll have until the light boys come at eight. Right?"

"Swell, Sam."

I watched him as he went about the organization of the stable morning. A word here, a gesture there. At one stall he stopped and stood for a long time without saying anything . . . like a man with nothing to do but look on. Then he walked away without a word to the groom who'd been working inside.

He stopped a black filly being led past by one of the ginnies, felt of a knee. "Hey, Doc." I walked over. "How long till I work this one?"

I poked around the knee. Home again. It was one of those knees . . . I said . . .

"You can work her right now, if she's fit, Sam."

"I would've waited, but I'll take your word for it, Doc."

"Thanks. But maybe there's a catch to it."

"How come?"

"You can work the filly this morning. You can put her right back on her schedule. Maybe she'll stand up for you and maybe she won't. But I can tell you one thing. That knee's not going to get any better while she's standing around here and getting light training."

"You mean if she doesn't stand up now she won't at all."

"That's right. If she's worth a lot of dough to you, send her back to the farm for a year right now. That might do it."

"I see. And if she isn't worth a lot of dough to me?"

"She'll make a beautiful saddle-mare for some society dame to canter around the Park."

Sam grinned and wandered over to the foreman. "You heard what the Doc said, Slim, breeze her half a mile with the last set and we'll see how she pulls up."

Sound cruel? It isn't at all. The tremendous shock of racing speeds is so great that legs which could pound through the hunting field all day, but are still unsound, simply won't take it. Filly is called Blackstar. You might watch for her. She'll possibly race for seasons before you see her in the Park.

Sam came back. "Okay, Doc. Thanks for the vetting. Now what's on the docket?"

"It's kind of serious. Where can we talk?"

"How about a cup of coffee? We can talk over at the shack."

Sam, I guess, took it for granted that when I'd said the talk was to be serious, I meant it. He seemed thoughtful and didn't say anything as we walked between barns to the lunch wagon. I was pretty thoughtful, myself. The place was quiet except for a group of exercise boys who piled out pushing either other around shortly after we sat down. It's a wonder race-horses live to grow up.

The counterman brought the coffee and we carried it to a dismal booth in the corner. "Well, Doc?"

I plunged. "Sam, through a set of circumstances which may or may not be of any importance to you, I've got myself into a position where I have to ask your advice on what may turn out to be a rather touchy subject."

"Why sure, Doc, why not?"

"Well, one reason why not is that it's a little personal . . . personal to both of us. Another is that I may be mixing up in something which is not only none of my business but which might give some people the wrong impression . . . might even prove dangerous for me."

"Tell me about it." Sam took a cinder out of his coffee. "If it has anything to do with me personally, I can't see how it could be dangerous for you. If it's personal with me and none of your business, Doc, I'll say so."

"Okay. That suits me. Look, Sam, you know, of course, about Harry Lennen's death."

Sam didn't jump or stare or fumble. He didn't do anything but say "Yes. I knew he was killed. Why?"

"It would be helpful if you knew anything about him. A very good friend of mine has been . . . what shall I say? . . . embarrassed by his death."

"Yes?"

"Yes. I was asked to see if I could find out more about the circumstances of his death . . . or of his former life . . . or any thing. Any thing I could find out without the knowledge of the police."

"Why without the knowledge of the police, Doc? You haven't got yourself on the other side of the law, have you?"

"I'm not exactly sure whether I have or not. If I have, it's been accidental. I'm quite sure the cops wouldn't like me running around putting my nose into their affairs. I'm certainly not working for them. I'm simply trying to help this friend out of a spot which I have every reason to believe he shouldn't be in."

"He, Doc?"

"Are you guessing, Sam?"

"No. I see the papers. I haven't talked with Gladys for some time, but I know she's in trouble over this thing. I took it for granted it wasn't too serious for her, personally, and that I'd better stay away unless she sent word she needed me."

"I see. Yes, it was Gladys . . . Terry as I'm more apt to think of her. The kid is getting a lot of attention from the cops and she's scared, Sam. Why did you take it for granted that it wasn't too serious for her personally?"

I think Sam did look a little upset at this. Maybe I'm wrong. Maybe he was thinking about her reputation . . . not her safety. Anyway he said, "I don't know why I took that for granted. I guess I just took for granted that Gladys isn't the sort of person to do a thing like that."

"She isn't."

"Then you'll understand how I felt."

Nice, comfortable ground . . . talking to Sam Eckman about his little daughter isn't the sort to commit a murder. Nobody gets hurt. Talking to him about how come she's been living with the cheap character that got killed is quite different. There didn't seem to be any easy way around it, so I jumped in.

"How much did you know about Lennen, Sam?"

He gave me a look. I felt like I'd reached into the potato-bag and got hold of a toad. "I didn't know him."

That was all. Both of us knew it was a lie . . . and both of us knew there would be nothing more said on the subject. Whatever Eckman knew about Harry Lennen wasn't pretty.

We called over for another cup of coffee. I wasn't getting anyplace and it didn't look as though I was going to. What's the use of asking Sam if he'd ever been at Lennen's place when I knew damned well he had. I didn't dare bring up Jocko Burns . . . he hadn't been mentioned any time in the whole case. I could easily drop a careless crack in the wrong spot and Jocko would turn up either in the jailhouse or the morgue. I tried another tack.

"Sam. In the last few weeks have you heard . . . or even sensed . . . any kind of a racing or bookmaking deal around? A betting coup or anything of that sort?"

"You know better than that, Doc, as long as you've been around the horses. You don't hear of that sort of thing. Or at least you hear about so-called coups that are supposed to have come off. Most of them are phony, of course. I still can't see why you have to play detective in order to help Gladys. It's damned nice of you but does she need it?"

"Yes. She does. I was probably a chump to get mixed up in it, but I am . . . and that's that. The only reason I'm playing detective is that I've got myself so involved I'll have a hell of a time squaring myself as it is."

"So you know a lot more than you've said." I didn't like the expression on Sam's face as he glanced at me over his cup. "What do you know?"

"Nothing that would hurt the killer and nothing, I'm sorry to say, that will help Gladys."

"Is her position any worse than the papers say?"

"Yes"

"Oh? How?"

Now what? I decided to go a little further. "Terry . . . Gladys had a call from Lennen the night he was killed. He wanted to talk to her. When she went to his place Lennen was dead. She might have simply called the police but there was a reason why she couldn't."

"What was that, Doc?"

"Can't you guess, Sam?"

"How could I guess?"

"I thought you might."

"I don't know what you're talking about."

"Okay, Sam, suppose we leave it this way. You want to spare Gladys any trouble you can over this thing, don't you?"

"Of course."

"I may have to come to you in the next day or two and tell you she needs your help very badly. It will involve the police. Will you help her?"

"Naturally."

"Even at the cost of some personal . . . embarrassment?"

"Yes." He didn't question the personal embarrassment angle.

"Right, Sam. Thanks for the time. I'll be getting along."

We got up and I paid the check. As we stood for a moment on the gravel path in front of the lunch wagon,

I asked him, quite suddenly, "Know anybody by the name of Pinky, Sam?"

He took a deep breath. His look was a take as they call it in show business . . . in pictures . . . he took it big. Then he said, "Doc, you're a nice guy. From all I hear, you're a fine doctor and have the respect of a lot of people. I understand you had the start of a nice practice before the war and that you did a swell job during the war. Don't you think it would be a pretty sound idea for you to stick to that instead of getting tangled up with the wrong people? I know you like to hang out with the theatrical and sporting crowd . . . and that's okay. But there are some situations connected with those businesses that get people in a lot of trouble . . . that get people hurt. Those are bad situations, Doc, for a fellow like you. Maybe it's none of my business . . . but there it is."

As I walked out the gate looking for a cab, I wondered whether I'd got a piece of friendly advice . . . or a particularly nasty threat.

8

I climbed out of the Eighth Avenue subway at Broadway and glanced over my shoulder at the dirty building which housed Harry Lennen's dirty apartment and which, undoubtedly, held the answer to a dirty murder. No signs of life. Eddie Marsh and his stalwarts had, by this time, combed out of that welter of mean odds and ends everything which might add the smallest fact to the story.

As I passed a fruit stand I drank a glass of what passed for orange juice, rejected the idea of further breakfasting and headed for home.

So Sam Eckman had proved either barren or uncommunicative. I might have forced the Pinky issue a little more and made certain whether Sam's small sermon had been a warning. It might have worked, and it might, also, have set off the fireworks. People who find they have hit other people lethally with milk bottles aren't apt to be too particular about their future relations with people who know about it. Sam might have done it himself . . . he'd been on the scene . . . but equally possible, he might be involved in it to the point where he'd be just as unhealthy to fool with.

There was nothing in the lobby mail box. The janitor hadn't been around yet. There were cigarette butts and a beaten-up comic magazine on the elevator floor. I'd have a leisurely shower and maybe call Katie and . . .

. . . there were four cigarette butts in the corner where the little let-down operator's stool was. The stool was down, too. Ordinarily when the car was on automatic it would be up. Funny.

. . . I'd make a date with Katie, maybe for lunch. She could get away sometimes . . .

The elevator bounced to a stop and I opened the door. The comic book lay just alongside the stool. It finally penetrated my vague wonderings that somebody had waited there in the elevator, last night. Had waited four cigarettes' worth and had amused himself with Superman. Last night? I'm quite certain they hadn't been there when I went out this morning at about six. Oh well . . .

However, my cigarette butt and comics man ceased to be of casual interest and became the center of the picture a moment later. The first thing I saw when I walked into the apartment was a large cop. He was standing flatfooted in the middle of the room and had all the earmarks of a guy looking for trouble.

I think I said "Well, hello!" or something equally appropriate. He said, "You Doc Connor?" When I allowed as how, he grunted and nodded his head toward the office. "The lieutenant wants to see you."

Oh. Oh.

Eddie Marsh was snooping around the place, sniffing like a hound. I said good morning and grinned. Eddie wasn't having any.

"Where have you been?"

"Out at Empire looking at the horses. What goes?"

"What time did you leave here?"

"About six o'clock, why? Is this a raid?"

"The raid was earlier. You've had visitors."

"The hell I have. When."

"Probably shortly after you left. The janitor tried to get the elevator, then walked up and saw them . . . or, at least he saw the one waiting in the elevator. When the janitor tried to question him, the guy locked him up in the broom closet. The scrub woman let him out at seven-thirty or so."

"Well! Well! What did they get?"

"Nothing as far as I can see. I was waiting for you."

"I'll look around."

"That's nice of you. Damn you, Doc, why can't you mind your own business? You know as well as I do that this isn't a routine burglary."

"Why not?"

"Lots of things."

"Such as?"

"Such as this rather handy fifty dollar bill here in plain sight on your desk."

"That . . ." I gargled . . .

"Sure. You leave money lying around and the guy doesn't even touch it! Burglary! This fellow was looking for something, and that something, Doc, has to be connected with the Lennen business. This is no coincidence. What was he looking for?"

"I wouldn't have the foggiest idea, Eddie . . . that's the truth. There's not a thing in my apartment or my office that could have the slightest bearing on the case . . ."

"Didn't you tell me you'd treated Lennen once?"

"Of course . . . wait."

I looked in the file. The Lennen card was there. Eddie Marsh said lessee and I showed it to him. He studied it while I thought of the old X-ray. That was there too. Eddie handed the card back.

"Nothing here," he grunted. "What else, Doc? There's bound to be something."

"Nothing, Eddie. Nothing. There can't be anything. You're crediting me with entirely too much on the Lennen thing. I can't believe this had anything to do with it."

"All right, Doc. Have it your own way. Can you check your narcotics?"

"That's something. I'm pretty finicky about opiates and don't keep much around." I went to the case. "There's your answer. A full tube of morphia quarters." I checked my bag. "Yes, and almost another full one from the bag."

"Anything else?"

I gave a quick look through the bag. My bag hypodermic outfit was there but it gave me an idea. I looked at the case again and found a new syringe and a box of needles missing. I told Marsh and he said he guessed that wrapped it up. A little while later Eddie sent the cop away and I hoped he would go himself but he hung around. I offered him a drink and he made a crack about morning drinking and continued wandering around the apartment. Finally he came out with it.

"If I'm not invading this mysterious new privacy of yours too badly, Doc, I'd kind of like to know what Sam Eckman had to offer this morning."

"Good Lord, Eddie, are you guys tailing me? You're wasting the city's money if you are."

"Look, Doc. I don't have to be a Sherlock Holmes to know that Terry Hale's father is at Empire and that you have undertaken to do something . . . probably ill-advised . . . for the girl and that you wouldn't be at Empire but at Aqueduct visiting Mr. Fitz if you wanted to hang around the track. What did Sam say?"

"He claims he didn't know Lennen, and that he hasn't heard of any betting coup, planned or otherwise which might account for the ten thousand dollars. Otherwise he said nothing."

"Nothing, eh?"

"He told me I ought to be minding my own business instead of getting mixed up with the wrong people."

"I salute a fellow breath-waster." Eddie sighed and reached for his hat. "I'm not making enough progress to keep everybody happy, Doc. I've got to get around to you by tomorrow and it may not be too pleasant if you've got anything very vital. So far there's been enough routine stuff to keep our minds off you. Stick around."

"Sure, Eddie, I know. You don't think I'm damned fool enough to involve myself in anything criminal, do you?"

"Not intentionally."

"That's white of you."

"Don't get me wrong, Doc. I think you're damned fool enough to do anything you thought was honest . . . whether other people thought so or not . . . and that takes in a lot of territory. See you tomorrow."

I watched his bulk crowd into the elevator and sent him down with a cheerier word than my general state suggested. I couldn't believe it was a routine morphine burglary either. You see the fifty dollar bill wasn't mine. I don't know why I hadn't told Eddie. It didn't make any sense not to, yet when you get involved in this business of trying to deceive a guy as smart as the lieutenant you have to think several times before you speak.

I wandered around the office again and checked things over. Nothing was in disorder. Whoever broke in had a fairly definite idea of where doctors kept things and went directly for them. Whoever broke in wanted some morphine and a new syringe. Most significant of all, whoever broke in left fifty bucks to pay for it. No addict . . . at least not the sort I'd seen. Could be, though. Why would anyone else steal it . . . complete with syringe?

I checked my bag again . . . I don't know why . . . and I found something that did make sense. My entire supply of sulfathiazole tablets was gone! What goes here? Morphia . . . hypodermic . . . sulfathiazole . . . that's no addict. That's got to be somebody with a sick person on his hands . . . a sick person who can't call a doctor. Sick people who can't call doctors are criminals. Logically, then, the occupational disease among criminals being gunshot wounds, I could guess the answer to my burglary with some degree of certainty. Doctors have to report gunshot wounds as a matter of police routine. So.

But why me?

I was extremely glad I hadn't followed up the thing while Eddie Marsh was around. I felt pretty certain that, someway, the burglary had to do with the Lennen murder. It couldn't be unrelated. I've said that things happen to you around my end of town . . . but not that fast. I put the fifty in an envelope for further reference. They might want to try it for prints or something after I had landed myself in the clink for complicity.

Katie was busy. I didn't like the race-card for the day. As far as detecting was concerned, Eddie Marsh could have it. I was sick of it to my innermost depths. I spent the afternoon watching a mental parade of ill-assorted facts that wouldn't fit together.

Jocko Burns, tout and bookmaker, discovers a corpse . . . or creates one. He rushes to me because he can't call the police, or thinks he can't. The corpse is a guy known to Broadway as Harry Lennen. He's a hanger-on wherever gambling is general. Terry Hale has been his girl and was to meet him at his apartment but finds him dead. She sees her father, Sam Eckman, a horse trainer, walking away from the building as she arrives. Sam Eckman suspiciously denies knowing Lennen, although we know he was in or at that building the night Lennen was killed. Last person known to have been with Lennen before his death, someone by the name of Pinky. All I know for sure is that the guy was good and dead around ten that night. If Terry's story of the telephone call was true, he was good and alive at about eight-thirty. The police say he was killed at some time around nine. On top of that, somebody was there around ten doing something . . . or bent on doing something . . . besides slugging me over the head.

If Jocko Buras and Terry Hale were telling the truth, Sam Eckman looked like the killer. Somehow I resisted that. I think it would have made more sense if Sam had headed that weird parade of innocents across the corpse. Maybe he had. Maybe he'd seen Terry and beat it.

What the hell! You can't just go 'round and 'round. If Sam killed Lennen it all makes sense. All we have to do is find out why. I can't see it that way, though.

I was just starting to call Katie again about five when the phone rang in my face. It was Eddie Marsh.

"Doc. I'm getting damned tired of acting like a conspirator in this case on account of you."

"Sorry. What now, Eddie?"

"You've got me calling you from pay-stations because I'm afraid to use the department board . . . but this is the last. Do you hear?"

"Sure, fella, but . . ."

"No good. This is the payoff. Tomorrow morning you'll be down here at nine and . . ."

"Nine . . . not nine . . ."

"Nine . . . sharp . . . or else. You'll come down here and unload. I'd bring you down here tonight only I've got some people coming in the morning for you to look at. Will you be there or will I send for you?"

"I'll be there, Eddie. As a matter of fact I'm getting a little scared of the thing myself."

"Scared? Why?"

"I'll tell you in the morning. It's nothing violent."

"Okay. Be sure you do. Now listen, Doc. I want you to make me a promise and it's important."

"What?"

"I want you to promise me that you'll make no attempt to get in touch with Terry Hale tonight . . . and that if she gets in touch with you, you'll keep your mouth shut and make no further attempt to cover her."

"Can you tell me why, Eddie?"

"Will you promise that?"

"Sure . . . if it's important."

"It's as much as my job is worth if you don't. It's that important. I want your solemn promise."

"Right, Eddie . . . you've got it." I could almost hear Eddie sigh with relief. It must have been important. "Can you tell me why?"

"I shouldn't, but now that you've agreed to behave yourself, I will. I'm going to bring Hale in in the morning . . . for keeps."

"No! She couldn't have done it!"

"Oh she couldn't! How do you know?"

"Hell, Eddie, actually I don't. I just don't think so."

"Great! I'll turn her loose on that. Anyway I'm not charging her yet but I'll bet you and Katie a dinner she's it before I get through."

"Maybe I'm wrong, but I'll take that." Eddie sounded certain. I suppose it was stupid not to believe him then and there, but I couldn't believe the girl had had any part in it. "What have you got against her?"

"Plenty. I not only believe she killed Lennen but I believe she must have rehearsed it with him . . . or something." He faltered a little at that one.

"Have you lost your mind?"

"Practically . . . but it still has to be that way. I guess you know that there were no positive prints on the milk bottle Lennen was killed with."

"That's what it said in the paper."

"Well, there weren't . . . but listen to this! I've got *another* milk bottle, picked up in the bedroom, which not only has her prints on it, but the laboratory actually found minute particles of scalp, a hair or two and bloody stains! Not much, but enough. What do you think of that?"

I didn't tell him what I thought of that.

9

I spent the next few minutes with the hand mirror trying to engineer some light on the back of my head. Sure enough there was a small cut that had bled a little. Hair and bloodstains on the milk bottle . . . and Terry Hale's prints. Oh brother! I'd better have another look at this case!

So Terry had sneaked away from her crowded dance hall very soon after she got there and come back to Lennen's apartment. There couldn't be much doubt about what she came back for. She was after that package she couldn't find . . . or didn't have time to find . . . the first time. Ten thousand dollars is a lot of dimes!

Beyond trying to get hold of Jocko who was out and didn't call back, half expecting a call from Terry, hoping for a call from Katie who was also out, I did nothing until bed time. I didn't relish the prospect of the morning downtown and I tried to organize the things I'd say. One thing sure . . . I'd start with Terry's visit and tell them to call her in so I could let her tell her own story. If they wouldn't do that, I'd have to tell them anyway. Equally sure I wasn't going to disclose my Lennen visit . . . and, of course, Jocko's call . . . until I had to. I felt that Terry would be better off to talk. I couldn't figure what she had to lose, as long as Sam Eckman seemed so unconcerned. I wondered if, by hesitating to admit my corpse stalking, I wasn't protecting the key figure in the whole affair . . . Burns.

'Round and 'round.

Katie called, as she does on rare occasions, at midnight. It made up for a rough day . . . more than made up for it because she was worried about me.

"Hello, darling, are you all right?"

"Of course, my sweet. Look what I've got to stay all right for." It's as bad as that sometimes. "What about you?"

"I'm sort of worried about you. I keep reading the paper about the . . . the thing . . . and wondering. I haven't seen anything about the telephone-exchange-five-lines business yet."

"You will tomorrow."

"Oh? It's come out then."

"It will. I'm due to sing at nine in the morning. A special audition for Eddie Marsh and a selected group."

"Jimmy! Will it be bad?"

"It won't be good, I'm afraid, my sweet."

"I knew something awful was happening. I could feel it in my bones!"

"There isn't a bone in your body. You're all soft and pokey like a . . ."

"Jimmy! Don't be revolting. You pick the damnedest ways of being gallant."

"How? Gallant?"

"Nobody in the world but you would think of calming a frightened woman by making her throw up. I hope they jail you. Night!"

Oh Katie, Katie, Katie!

It was one-thirty when I got to bed. It was two-thirty when I got to sleep. It was three-thirty when I woke up with a flashlight in my face, a bitter fear in my heart and a strange, hard voice in my ears.

"Okay, Doc, wake up!" My heart exploded inside me. "Wake up, Doc, you're goin' on a hurry call."

I struggled to the top for a breath. I suppose I could have thought I was back in St. Vincent's and was wanted down in Emergency. I could have thought I was back at Iwo . . . or Saipan. I could have thought I was anyplace I'd ever been in my life. But I didn't. I thought I was in bed in Forty-eighth Street and a guy . . . maybe two guys . . . wanted me to get up and go someplace I didn't want to go. I could have thought I wasn't scared, too.

"Come on, Doc, get goin' . . . we ain't got all night."

"What's the matter? Take the light out of my eyes!" He did. I shook my head a couple of times and did a little fast thinking. This is the Lennen thing, of course. Visions of Eddie Marsh and those stalwart blue uniforms tantalized me like a mirage. Maybe I could get this guy to tell me more about it. He couldn't shoot me for asking. He couldn't, eh?

"Listen, fella, I don't know what this is all about . . ."

"You gotta see a patient, Doc. Don't ask no more questions. Just get goin'. Don't reach for the light. I'll give you the flash where you need it. Get dressed."

I got dressed . . . trying to think hard and getting no place. In the darkness back of the blinding beam I sensed another man. He didn't speak or move. Just stood there. I also sensed that he was the boss. No threat of violence . . . the whole thing even had a sort of conciliatory tone. Yet, from the moment I wakened I knew there was no use arguing or trying to make a break. It was smooth, experienced and efficient. The finger in my sleeping ribs might as well have been a gun.

Suddenly it put itself together. It had to be a gunshot wound. It had also to be my visitors of this morning. The guy had left fifty dollars on the desk. It was somebody in a jam . . . an illegal jam . . . a spot which, in his mind, justified extreme measures . . . yet he left fifty bucks to square himself. At least this fellow will be fair according to his standards. I felt a little relieved. Not much. I tied my shoe laces and stood up.

"Okay, boys, now what?"

The voice from the darkness cut in for the first time and the man with the light stood aside. I was startled at the quiet, normal quality of the man's speech.

"There's no time, now, for apologies, Doc. We've got a man on our hands with a slug in his belly and we need help. I've done what I can for him . . ."

"Morphia and sulfathiazole."

"That's right, Doc . . . yours."

"Thanks for the fifty."

"Let's not kid around. This fellow is probably dying."

"He needs immediate surgery. You've got to hospitalize him."

"You don't tell me what I've got to do, Doc, I tell you what you've got to do. Yes. Of course he needs surgery. Get what is necessary and let's go."

"Good God, man! I haven't the stuff to do that sort . . ."

"Bring what you have and get going. If you haven't got it we'll get it for you someway."

That was all there was to it. I'd have to argue later if there was any arguing to be done. A man with a slug in his belly is not a pretty risk even with perfect care . . . and I knew that the best I could do would be to sit around and watch the guy die . . . or kill him on a kitchen table in some hideout. The man with the flash followed me around while I gathered up what I could. I had a pretty fair layout of instruments but most of them were still stored. Finally I said, "This is the best I can do. We might as well go."

We went. They watched me lock the door and one waited in the darkened elevator. They'd turned the hall light off as well. We went down. I kept having recurrent flashes of doubt as to the real reason for this expedition. I knew that somebody . . . one person out of the people whose names had come up in connection with Lennen, or even someone new, wanted me out of the way. I reassured myself with the thought that they went to a lot of trouble, if that was the case, to put on a show of stealing my drugs. No. There had to be a patient. Maybe it was both.

I thought of Eddie Marsh and the scene which would come off in his office at Headquarters in the morning. Man oh man! It would hardly occur to Marsh that anything had happened to me . . . feeling as he did at the moment. Or would it? I had told him I was a little scared about some of the developments . . . but I hadn't told him what or why. I couldn't look for much help from Eddie for some time.

When we got to the lobby floor, I found myself facing the elevator door with my back to the two men. Before the door was opened, a voice behind me said, very quietly, "It is to your advantage, Doctor, if you don't make any attempt to recognize us. Please walk between us and a little in front. There's a car at the corner . . . to the right. Let's go."

Between the apartment house door and the corner we met three people . . . a shabby woman, a man with a bucket and window-washing equipment and a well-dressed young chap who was very drunk. As we came to the car the voice said again, "Just keep your back turned, Doc. We have no intention of manhandling you. Pull your hat over your eyes."

I did. Why not? I didn't want to see them just then either. One of them gave the brim a solid pull for good measure and I got into the back seat. One of the men got in with me and closed the door. The other went around to the driver's seat and I heard the starter, the motor, the gears and we rolled down Forty-eighth Street. I decided to try to count turns and estimate mileage. We went several blocks and turned left. That would be North . . . Forty-eighth is West to East. Probably we were on Lexington. The hat was very tight and uncomfortable. After a few more blocks . . . I think five, we turned right. That might be . . . no it had to be four because we turned East. Had to be an even numbered street. That would be Fifty-second. We went what seemed three blocks. We turned right. I had just figured out Fifty-second and First Avenue when I heard a little chuckle beside me. "How close do you make it, Doc?"

"How close do I make what?"

"We're at First Avenue and Fifty-second Street. I just wondered how close you'd got to it."

I had nothing to say. I didn't feel like playing games just then. But I quit counting. They'd lose me. The head man took care of that immediately afterward by starting a one-sided conversation. I found myself listening with great care.

"I know you want all this the nice way, Doc, as nice, at least, as we can make it under the circumstances. We do too. We figure you'd be able to get out of almost any kind of a hole . . . what with your friends around here and in Center Street. Any kind of a hole that a fellow like you'd be apt to get in. We think that, if you had to tell the cops you were forced to attend to a gunshot wound, that you didn't know where you were and that you didn't recognize any of the people, you'd not be questioned too much. Now we're in quite a different position. We haven't many friends around here, and none at all in Center Street. We can't afford to draw attention to ourselves. The point I'm making is that you will have to stay with us for some time . . . until the patient is out of danger. I won't even take into consideration the idea that he won't get well. He will . . ."

"But look here . . ."

"I know, Doc. Forget that. We'll try. Again, the point is that you'll be around for some time. You can make that time as easy or as difficult as you want for yourself. From what I've heard of you, you'll take care of the patient first and worry about your freedom second. That true?"

"I suppose so . . . I've never been in a situation like this before. I wouldn't know. I suppose so."

"You took care of guys in the war, didn't you, when you had to risk your life to do it?"

"That's different."

"Maybe . . . maybe not. What I'm trying to explain to you is that all you have to do is to get tough and we all lose . . . you, of course, more than we. On the other hand, one of us is hurt . . . badly. He's going to have proper medical attention . . . or, at least as proper as the circumstances permit. We'll gamble our safety without question. We are quite willing, also, to gamble *your* safety on the same thing. Make sense, Doctor?"

According to his viewpoint it did make sense and I told him so. In his conversational way he said, "We can't stop to choose viewpoints. With things as they are, I'm afraid you'll have to look at things our way for a while." I thought this over before I spoke again.

"It's all very logical, as I see it . . . despite the fact that you've taken the trouble to put it nicely. If I go along and take care of the patient and mind my own business while I'm your . . . guest . . . I live to take care of my friends' hangovers again in the future. If not, I give up my life in the interest of ethics

. . . ethics of doubtful worth where a really hurt human being is involved. Right?"

"Perfectly," he said. He added, "Sorry."

We rode on in silence. We had turned many times. Once in a while there would be street sounds but mostly just the vagrant, occasional motors and horns which make New York at four in the morning sound like any other city. Once there was a switch-engine whistle, fairly close. The windows of the car were all rolled up and sounds were vague. That hat was very uncomfortable.

We passed a toll gate. Money changed hands. It could have been either a bridge or a tunnel. Hudson to New Jersey? George Washington Bridge? Lincoln to Bergen . . . or South? Or North? Or a blind? Maybe it had been the Midtown to Long Island. As I was foolishly trying to remember the pitch of the register bell, the man beside me whistled a tune, softly, off key.

We must have been on the road an hour when we slowed down and the driver said, "What about it, boss?" My companion said, "It's okay, drive in."

We drove on a few hundred yards and stopped. Someplace near us there was music of sorts . . . a bad small combination such as you hear in third-rate roadhouses. They were playing *Stardust*.

There was some maneuvering around with the car again and, as we pulled up finally, the man said, "This is it, Doc. You will go in and up some steps. We'll lead you. Don't trying anything and you'll be curing your friends' hangovers before long." He added. "I have your bag."

We crawled out of the car and crossed a small, uneven patch of ground. We climbed wooden steps. They were outside steps . . . perhaps to a second-floor porch. A few level paces and we stopped. The boss, on my right, opened a door and we went into some sort of room or hall. It smelled of kitchen odors . . . not too unpleasantly. Like the back door of a clean restaurant. The music droned along, apparently directly below us. Country roadhouse. Laughter down there . . . one woman and some men. We stood for a moment, waiting. The boss went on ahead for something. The music came to a dismal stop. I heard the familiar clank and the repeated clicks of a slot machine . . . a rattle of coins and a male shout. Roadhouse all right. I could use a drink.

The boss came back after a while and they led me forward to another door. Down my nose, under the hat, I could see light and an inch or two of floor. The boss spoke.

"Okay, Doc, here you are. You're next door to your patient . . . there's a bathroom between you. I've provided the few things you'll need . . . razor, pajamas, and some clean linen. I think they'll fit. Your meals and anything you'll need for your patient will be brought up from downstairs. I'm locking the doors from the outside but there's an old call bell on the wall which rings in the kitchen below. If you need me, use it. Okay?"

"I guess it'll have to be. I'd like to get rid of this damned hat."

"Why not? Here's your bag . . . then I'll beat it and you'll be . . . what do you call it? . . . resident physician."

"Interned."

He laughed. "For the moment you aren't just kidding, Doc. Here you are."

He set the bag at my feet. Down my nose I saw his hand and wrist against the black leather. They were covered with pink hair.

Pinky on five!

10

Well, I was looking for him, wasn't I?

I pulled off the hat and rubbed my forehead and nose. A febrile moan from the adjoining room reminded me that I had things to do and I looked around. It was a routine country hotel bedroom . . . possibly a cut better than most. Decent maple furniture and a comfortable looking bed with a spread that matched the curtains. On the table beside the bed was a bottle of Forester, some ice and a glass. Well. Well. The guy, while robbing my apartment, had noted my brand of whiskey. Might be a hard man to outsmart. Right then I didn't much feel like trying it.

The bathroom, as I walked through seemed surprisingly modern and was very clean. The room beyond was almost exactly like mine. On the bed lay the patient . . . a young fellow. His skin was dark and he had a small, turned-up nose. I took his hand. It was large for his size, and hard. It was also burning up. His pulse was sound . . . but characteristic. I pulled the covers back and lifted his pajama shirt. The wound had been bandaged with reasonable skill and gauze sponges provided an absorbent pad over the mess. The boy was thin.

I covered him up and went back to my room.

He looked like a jockey . . . maybe a little big . . . but whatever else he was, he was an awfully sick kid with a screaming temperature and a negligible chance to live. A country road-house is no place for a well-established peritonitis. I rang the bell. Pinky came at once.

"Yes, Doc?" He stayed outside the door.

"This boy can't stay here. He's got to go to a hospital."

"I knew that yesterday. The point is he can't go to a hospital. That's what you're here for. Get that through your head. He can't go anywhere but right here . . . and nobody's going to see him but you!" Pinky spoke patiently enough but he sounded as though he might be getting a little tired of repeating himself.

"He's got to have surgery. Proper surgery, not the kitchen-table sort. He's got to have it right away. His chances are damned bad under the best circumstances . . . this thing's gone too long. If I operate here with what facilities I've got, I'll kill him."

"And if you don't, the fellow who shot him will have killed him. That's a fine point of ethics . . . but I see it." His voice got strained and hard. Ugly. "I can't make you do the operation at the point of a gun, but I can come damned close to seeing that you'll never do another one. I'd heard that you were the kind of a guy who'd have guts enough to do the best job you could under any circumstances."

"You don't scare me a bit with that." I was sore, not brave. "I was scared before, but I'm goddamned if I am now. I'm not hollering for *my* life, you stupid lug, I'm hollering for the boy's life. You stand out there talking ethics with me and all the time you're saving your own skin because you haven't got guts enough to let me do what's right for the kid! Okay! Have them put on all the kettles they've got down there, clean and full of water and boil them . . . boil hell out of them. Find me the brightest light fixture in the place and all the clean sheets you can lay your hands on. Now, for the love of God, get away from here and let me think!"

I suppose that's about what I said. Maybe I've toned it down a little. It's what I meant anyway. I wasn't scared of Pinky any more. But I was afraid of the nasty, incompetent job I was about to do. I turned away, sick, from the door, when I heard Pinky's voice again.

"Thanks, Doc. It may help us get along a little better for you to know that I'm not saving my own skin, as you call it. I'm saving the boy's. I'd rather have him die here, under your care, than have him die in the chair for something he didn't do." I heard the hall floor squeak as he turned away. "Thanks, again, Doc. I'll get the stuff ready."

I went back to see the boy. He was still asleep and his pupils showed where at least some of my morphia had gone. I wondered how much sulfathiazole he'd been given and how much good it might, possibly, do him. Chances are, not much. I went back to my room, looked at the Forester bottle, put it away and washed my hands. I began laying stuff out of my bag.

The music had stopped and I remembered a car or two roaring away from the place. Somewhere below a lonely sort of voice was singing *Only a Shanty on Old Shantytown*. That I suppose, would be a dish-washer. If I were a dish-washer at a joint like that, I'd sing that way I think.

I was lonely as hell. If the Old Doc could have been there it would have been something else . . . a challenge or something. He'd have muddled through it as he had so many country emergencies. Muddled through? Dammit, no! He'd have done the thing right with all the wrong equipment. He would have called it inconvenient!

There wasn't much else to do about it, so I got out the thermometer and the stethoscope and went back to the boy on the bed.

Pinky had come back after a while and had said, through the door again, that they'd done what I'd asked. They were boiling copper vessels in the kitchen, that they'd taken one of the spotlights from the dance floor and it could be set up anyplace, that they had plenty of clean sheets and towels. Now what would he do?

He was like a small boy, this great lug . . . even when I howled, "Then goddammit, we cut out this asinine monkey-business of yelling through doors! Get a mask on like a bandit or something. Later you or somebody's going to have to wear a mask like a surgeon. I can't do anything here. I want to come downstairs and figure this thing out."

"Okay, Doc. Come down in a minute. I'll get the guys out of the way." He left without locking the door.

I didn't wait. I followed almost on his heels . . . mad and scared. Standing there in the hall was Pinky . . . no mask . . . no nothing. I said, "Well! Well!"

He just stood there . . . solid, unsmiling. I had some smart and mean crack in front of my mind and dropped it. I said, "Thanks, Pinky."

If he was startled when I called him Pinky, he didn't show it. He simply said, "I guess we'll understand each other better from now on. Tell me what to do."

I told him and he did it. For more than two hours I told him . . . and he did it. Through all that nightmare of a morning he was everywhere. Pinky! Pinky on five!

Then we were ready . . . as ready as we'd ever be. Two café tables . . . long and solid, side by side. A brilliant dance-floor spotlight. Instruments sterilized in kitchen colanders for drainage. Anesthesia from a cone fashioned out of a strainer covered with gauze. It was a little like trying to fix a watch with a pair of pliers.

The bullet had entered the right lower abdomen and I made a rectus incision on that side. Pinky said, "Jesus!" I said, "Shut up! This is the kid's guts not yours. You'll need yours on that end. Steady!"

"Sorry, Doc."

"Okay, fella, there is something pretty personal about that first incision. Just hold it."

He said nothing and went back to his dripping. I fooled around with tying off bleeders longer than I dared, cursing my luck, then went on through the fascia with scissors. With forceps I picked up the peritoneum and incised it with the knife. It was a mess.

"I might have saved this boy yesterday."

Pinky just said, "Save him today, Doc."

The bowel had been punctured, just to make it tougher, and I was mopping around trying to repair it when I struck something. Hard, metallic. It was the slug. I started to toss it into the basin when I remembered what it might mean. I set it quietly aside with some dirty stuff and went back to work. When I'd got the bowel repaired and the drains set I started sewing him up. Pinky relieved from his task, stood back from the table sick and sweating. I said, "Good work," and told him I'd be through in a few minutes. The kid's respiration was bad but, hell . . . I couldn't expect a miracle. Yet somehow I did expect one.

I cursed my way through the three rows of sutures and taped on a pad that would do until we could get the boy straightened out and into some breathable air. I was groggy as hell myself and Pinky had finally given up and was vomiting in the corner. I interrupted his retching.

"You've got the bed warmed?"

"Yes. Whiskey bottles filled with hot water from the sterilizers."

"Give me that blanket. Let's get this fellow out of here."

They'd found a canvas army cot which would serve for a stretcher. Pinky went to the door and called out and a couple of guys came in with gauze masks on their faces. I laughed. Pinky looked a little silly for a moment . . . then said, "I could hardly ask these boys to . . ."

I guess I laughed again and I said, "They look funny. Come on, boys, hold the cot up level while we slide him over." One of the slobs said, "Jeez! It smells awful in here. Will he live, Doc?"

I told him no. Pinky told him to shut up. The four of us got the boy upstairs and into his bottle-warmed bed. We lined the bottles up and down his sides and the two guys retreated.

Then Pinky laughed . . . pretty hysterically, I thought, for a tough guy. I told him he'd better go and clean himself up and get a little air . . . and what the hell was he laughing at?

"Okay, Doc, okay. I'm sorry I laughed. It wasn't funny. I was just thinking that the poor little bastard never took a drink in his life and now he's laid out to die that way . . . framed in whiskey bottles!"

11

I heard the door close behind Pinky and followed his foot-steps downstairs. There was a rumble of voices below and then quiet. I looked at my watch. Ten-fifty. There was a window in the patient's room but the shade was down. I raised it. Boards, solidly and neatly nailed. The shade undoubtedly was drawn as a matter of esthetics. Pinky again. I didn't bother to look at the window in my room.

The boy was alive and that was all. Heart, respiration, color just what I must have expected. He needed . . . he needed every-thing I didn't have to give him. I thought of great reserve sup-plies of plasma I'd seen in places where they hadn't been need-ed. I thought of spots I'd been where there hadn't been any. The kid would be badly dehydrated before evening and I'd want intravenous saline. Or would I need anything by then?

Ten-fifty! So sorry, Lieutenant Marsh, I'm two hours late to solve your murder for you. I'm visiting in the country. I won-dered what Eddie was thinking. I wondered what Katie would do when she found I was gone. She would call me to find out what happened at the nine o'clock meeting in Center Street. Then she'd call me again at dinner-time. Then she'd worry and call me from then on until she finally called Eddie Marsh.

I got feeling sorry for myself and went into the other room and had quite a slug of Forester. That, they tell me, is the un-failing symptom of the alcoholic. The whiskey made me tired. I went back to the boy's room and looked at him some more . . . I don't know why. I've seen horse trainers do that. They'll stand in front of a certain horse's stall for an hour at a time, simply looking at him. I asked Mr. Fitz, once, why, they did that and he said, "Well, I'll tell you, Doc, I've noticed that we don't spend nearly as much time standing in front of the good ones as we do the bad ones. These fellows can't tell you much that you can't see for yourself if you look long enough and, even if you don't know what you're looking for, you keep on looking for it."

"Even if you don't know what you're looking for, you keep on looking for it!" Man, you could write quite a hunk of essay on that, couldn't you! I stared at the little guy on the bed and wondered if he'd ever have anything to say to me. I wondered if I was looking for something that was stored up in that drug-numbed head. It occurred to me that he could easily have a lot of things in that head that Pinky didn't want me to know. If so, I might expect a call from that source with the first stirring of the patient. I turned off the ceiling light and lighted a bedside fixture before I left the boy. I brought the hypodermic syringe from my bag and some ampules I'd probably need and left them on the shelf in the bathroom. Then I rang for Pinky.

I heard the bell below, the sound of a muffled voice, some sort of an answer and, finally, steps on the stairway. Pinky walked in looking somewhat refreshed.

"Yes, Doc?"

"How do you feel?"

"Some better, thanks. I had a shower. How's the boy?"

"Alive."

"That's something, isn't it?"

"Not yet. There's a long way to go."

"By that I take it you mean he's got a chance."

"It was wishful thinking. I haven't a reason in the world to offer in support of his living through this mess. I have every reason to believe he won't. If I don't get some things from town today, I know he won't."

Pinky was silent a while. It suddenly occurred to me that I hadn't really taken a good look at him. He was big and square with a rugged, bony structure that showed plenty of power. His skin, milk-white and lightly freckled, looked clean and his eyes clear. The hair from which he got his name was sparse and definitely pink. I'd have taken him for about forty. His heavy, intelligent features were screwed up in a childishly worried expression as he puzzled over my request.

"Things from town. That's not easy, Doc."

"Nothing about this is easy. You want me to save the boy if it's possible. I've done everything I can so far. He's still alive. If he's alive in another few hours, I'll need things to keep him alive. There's got to be a way to get them . . . or we've been wasting our time. That's flat."

"Any suggestions?" Pinky grinned at the possibility of my making a suggestion.

"Nothing you'd accept . . . unless . . ."

"Unless what?"

"Unless you'd let me call a friend."

"You know I can't do that."

"You might get away with getting it yourself or have one of those gorillas of yours do it. I could give you an order for the stuff."

"That's out, too."

"Whose skin are you saving now?"

"Yours among others . . . shut up and let me think." After a moment he looked up. "Who's this friend you want to call?"

"A woman friend . . . Katie Storm. She's the only person I know who could be trusted to do exactly as I say . . . under these circumstances."

"The girl on the radio?"

"Yes."

"Is she your girl?"

"I wish she was. But I see what you mean. Yes, she thinks enough of me to do what I say without question if I convince her it's important."

"And you'd call her . . . where?"

"After you've thought about it you'll decide that you'd better call her instead of me. You'll call her at her office, explain that I want her to do something for me, then you'll put me on. I'll tell her that it's very important to me to get the stuff and that I

am in no immediate danger or trouble but that it is imperative
that she forget the fact that we called her."

"Then she'd leave the stuff someplace where I could pick it up."

"That's right."

"She'll do it, will she?"

"Yes."

Pinky scratched his head a couple of times and grinned at
me as though I'd given him a surprise raise in a poker game. He
got up and walked over to the window, absent-mindedly raising
the shade. The boards seemed to surprise him and he laughed.
Finally he sat down again and said, "Why not, Doc? I'm the guy
that decided you'd think of your patient before your own safety
. . . so I'm stuck with it."

It was my turn to grin. "Do you still believe it?"

"I guess I'm a little like you and your wishful thinking about
. . . about your position. I haven't got a reason in the world to
believe that a guy in your spot could . . . should be trusted. But
I can't help but think you'd be damned fool enough to call a
truce until the worst of this is over."

"It's a situation in which standard ethics . . . medical or personal either . . . fall down a little. I'm afraid, frankly, that the
youngster in there is going to die anyway . . . whatever we decide
to do. On the other hand, his only chance to live depends on medical supplies from town. The getting of those supplies involves
danger to you . . . and yours . . . if I should find a way to disclose
this location. If I attempt to get them without trying to notify
the law, I am doing less than my duty as a member of society."

Pinky looked quite thoughtful and not the least menacing.
He said, "Of course, Doc, while that's all true, there's another
angle you left out. You may have forgotten it . . . though I
doubt it." I asked him what that was without having to wonder
too much. I guess I just wanted to hear him say it. It was all
pretty matter-of-fact. "While you are considering ethics, medical and personal, you can't overlook the fact that, if you should
find a way to disclose this location . . . and you could, of course
. . . you'd run into quite a little trouble. You're still our . . .
guest . . . you know."

"That was nicer than most threats."

"It was intended to be." Pinky rose. "Suppose we get busy. Write out your instructions to the girl and let me see them. In the meantime I'll figure out a way to pick the stuff up." He started out and turned in the doorway. "By the way. When's the best time to call?"

I looked at my watch. "Within the next half hour."

"Right. I'll be ready." His steps moved down the hall, down the stairs, and I heard him speak to one of the men. A few minutes later I caught pieces of his voice, apparently on the telephone. A car pulled away from the place and I followed it out of hearing before turning to the business of the list. I can't tell you why, but I had no idea of trying to send any secret message. As a matter of fact I found myself figuring out ways of avoiding possible slips in the proposed plan. Maybe I'm lacking in civic sense or moral fiber or something. I don't believe I was frightened by Pinky's threats. Or was I?

I'm probably emotionally immature. This guy Pinky was getting under my skin and I kept having the feeling that he must be a right sort of a guy with something on his hands he couldn't handle any other way. Famous last words. In twenty minutes Pinky was back.

"Ready?"

I told him I was and we went downstairs and through a back hall to a room I hadn't seen. One door was closed, but, from its position, I guessed it led to the main room. It was sort of an office but everything had been cleared from the desk and nothing was in sight except a calendar, an ash tray and the telephone. Pinky closed the door behind him and said, "Sit down . . . here. Now. What's the number?"

I gave it to him, adding the extension. He wrote it down. He asked me just who would be expected to answer and for whom he'd ask . . . and how. He seemed to be very particular about that . . . as if he weren't too used to business telephones. Then he asked me what I would say. I told him. He told me what he would say to Katie before I spoke to her, and afterward. "Now," he said, "go back to the room where you did the operation and wait until I call you. Don't get funny. There's a guy back there to watch you."

I wondered about that moment until I remembered that he would have to give the operator his number . . . it must be a long-distance call. I had only been in the far room a minute or so when a voice startlingly close by said, "Okay, Doc, he wants you in there."

As I came in, he was saying, ". . . and the doctor has asked me to call you in this emergency. Just a moment, Miss Storm, here, is Dr. Connor now." He handed me the telephone.

"Katie?"

"Jimmy! Darling! I called you early this morning to tell you that Eddie Marsh . . ."

"Listen, Katie, I need your help. Very badly. I need your complete and absolute co-operation. No questions. Right?"

"Of course, Jimmy. Anything . . . naturally. But where are you? What's happened?"

"Quiet, my darling. Your job, right now, is to listen. Your job right now is to listen and do exactly as I say. It's terribly important. Will you?"

"Yes."

"Now get this straight. I am not calling you under any compulsion or by direction. I've got a very sick patient on my hands and I need some medicines for him. There's a reason why I don't want to have my whereabouts known to anybody. Not even you. Can I trust you to get the things I need if I give you a list?"

"Of course. Of course, Jimmy."

As I dictated the list I noticed for the first time that Pinky had left the room. I felt certain he was listening at an extension. I glanced at the dial on the phone I was using. The number disk had been removed. Katie read the list back to me and I got ready to sign off . . . adding . . . "Listen, sweet. Don't try to make any code or signal out of what I've said, or to try to find any hidden meaning in it. You won't find any. I simply want to save a patient's life. You must not say a word of this to anybody . . . no matter how long I'm away . . . understand?"

"Oh, yes. But I'm so . . ."

"I love you very much. I'm hanging up, now, and another man will tell you what to do with the things."

"I love you, too, Jimmy! But I'm frightened. You're in danger of some sort. Can't you tell me anything? Anything?"

"Don't worry, darling, I'm all right. There's nothing to tell you that won't keep until I get home . . ."

I was pretty sick about the whole thing and had started to hang up when I heard Pinky's voice from the extension . . . "Please don't be disturbed, Miss Storm. The doctor is doing a fine service to a man who needs help very badly and isn't in a position at the moment to get it in any other way. Let me assure you that the doctor is in no danger. For the moment he has given up his career as . . . er . . . detective to become the skilled physician he is. The only danger which could possibly come to him would be through your own error. May we count on you?"

I heard Katie say, "Of course." Then Pinky said, "Will you hang up, now, Doctor?" I hung up. That had been part of the plan . . . that I was not to hear the delivery instructions, although I hadn't known there would be an extension.

Oh Katie, Katie, Katie!

When I got up from the phone and tried the door, it was locked. A few minutes later Pinky turned the key and said, "All right, Doc, let's go back upstairs."

After we'd reached the room, Pinky sat down and lighted a cigarette. I walked through and took a useless look at the kid. He was stirring a little and I set a basin where I could reach it when I'd need it. I went back and sat where I could watch him through the bathroom. The Forester bottle suggested a drink and I asked Pinky if he'd join me. He said no thanks and I poured one for myself.

I thought about Katie and I guess Pinky thought about something or other because he didn't say anything. After a while I heard some pans rattle downstairs and somebody began to sing *Only a Shanty in Old Shantytown.*

12

It was a long haul. Pinky was in and out without much to say. He seemed nervous and under a lot of pressure. I don't wonder. Even I had no reason to believe that Katie hadn't taken things into her own hands and called Eddie Marsh. If she had, the next thing we could expect was two or three carloads of cops. I had no idea how Pinky and the other guys would greet them but I had an idea it wouldn't be pretty.

If the boy in the other room was slated for the chair he hadn't robbed anybody's piggy bank. He'd up and killed somebody. Probably Lennen, of course. If he had, where had the gun come from? The slug was safely in my pocket. Why it didn't go through the guy I don't know and the only person who'd ever find out exactly would be the surgeon, autopsy or otherwise, who followed me into his belly cavity. In a traumatic peritonitis, the lost and found articles department has to wait as a rule.

The slug seemed light. I'm not much of an authority on such things, but I'd say it was about a thirty-two. If Lennen had shot the boy somebody had carried off the gun. Whoever took it away had wanted the crime to look like a brutal murder and didn't want anyone associated with it. Perhaps he thought there was a chance nobody would be associated with it if the gun were hot there for the police. That theory would suggest that he had, of course, kept the gun as evidence in case it were ever needed.

On the other hand, that didn't jibe with Pinky's statement that the boy would die in the chair if he were caught. That would imply that Pinky didn't have the gun. I went on juggling the things I knew, trying to fit in the things I didn't know, but the whole thing didn't make any sense. Then I heard footsteps in the hall. Pinky knocked and walked in. He still looked damned serious to me, but he said, "Well, it looks as though they made it all right." He dropped down in the armchair. "Your patient still the same?" I told him the boy was no better . . . no worse . . . and he said, "I had arranged for my man to call me when he had the stuff and was sure he wasn't being followed. He just called."

"That's fine. I'll need the things badly by the time he gets here. I need them now." I was pretty curious to know how the delivery had been arranged and asked him.

"It was pretty simple . . . at least as simple as I could work it. After all, if Miss Storm was going to let us down, there wasn't much anybody could do to prevent the cops from following the stuff here. She could have had the call traced easily enough. We talked a sufficient length of time for somebody to call the police on another line."

"I felt certain she wouldn't have."

"Did you?"

"Absolutely."

"So did I, for some reason. She's all right."

"Did your man see her?"

"He saw her but not to talk to. He watched her do the things I'd instructed."

I checked myself from asking how she looked. "What had you told her to do?"

"Nothing very mysterious. When she had the supplies she was to get them into a taxicab, find a public telephone and hold the cab while she called a number. When she did that she was told to tell the cab driver that her car was parked at . . . as it turned out . . . Fiftieth and Sixth Avenue . . ."

I said, "Thoughtful."

Pinky grinned a little. "I looked up her broadcast. Well, she did all that, stowed the stuff in our car, and walked down Fiftieth without looking back."

"She never looks back . . . bless her heart."

"My man said she didn't. The rest was simple, but painful for him. He hasn't got as much faith in his fellow man as some of the rest of us. That's why I employ him. He simply drove into a public garage with which we've had some dealings and waited around to be arrested. He wasn't, so he called me and is on his way."

"I hope the stuff proves of some use."

Pinky got up and walked to the bathroom door. "I hope so, too, Doctor." He looked at the boy for a while. "Isn't it about time he got out from under the anesthetic?"

"He is out. I gave him some sedation; quite a lot. He's better off as he is. This isn't a routine case. It had gone too long. I'm not sure I had any business operating. Maybe your . . . my sulfathiazole has helped some."

"I didn't know what else to give him."

"If you had to give him anything except a break at a decent hospital, you did the right thing. It's of doubtful value in a mess like this."

"You'll need some rest, won't you? The cook's back for the night and I'll send up a tray. The food's pretty good as a rule . . . the usual roadhouse stuff . . . steaks, chops, oysters. At any rate, you can call your shots. The fried chicken is better than average."

"Thanks. I do need some rest and I suppose I'll be hungry before long. I'll get a shower and maybe by that time the supplies will have come. I'll need your help after that for a while. This fellow will have to be watched every minute from now on, too. I hope you'll be able to take a shift. How about your own rest?"

"I'll make it all right. Just tell me what you want done."

"I don't suppose there's a woman around you could trust."

"In that, Doc, I'm afraid you're the lucky one. I've not had much success at trusting women. I'm not a bad hand in a sickroom and I'd rather the two of us handled it alone . . . if it's okay with you."

"Sure. We can do it." I was getting sorry for the guy again. What sort of a code is this I'm learning? Here I am, the self-appointed God of Judgment, stalking the gent who knocked off

Harry Lennen, and all the time finding myself feeling sorry for the guys who probably did it. I heard a car drive into the yard. "Will that be the stuff?"

"Wait a second." He listened. The car turned into the back end and, in a moment, I heard the sliding of a garage door. "Yes. I'll have it up to you right away." Pinky disappeared in a hurry and I heard him clattering down the stairs like a kid at recess. His feet made the first cheerful sound I'd heard out of him since I'd known him.

I resumed my interrupted negotiations with the Forrester and went to the bathroom and started to scrub my hands. In the middle of it I had to rush to the boy's room and grab the basin. The boy's retching was mercifully light. I bathed his face and washed his mouth with a cold towel. As I turned away, Pinky was standing behind me. He said, "The stuff's in the other room. It's quite a package."

I said it would be and asked him if he could find me a clothes-tree somewhere downstairs and maybe an electric plate unless he wanted me fooling around the kitchen. He went off promising to find them both.

Katie had been, as usual, meticulous in carrying out instructions and everything was there . . . including a carton of Chesterfields and, believe it or not, a toothbrush. She could not have said more plainly in words that she knew I had not made the trip voluntarily. I searched carefully for some other message. There was none.

After a few minutes Pinky came back lugging a coatrack under one arm and an electric hotplate slung over his back by the cord. "These do, Doc?" He was positively cheerful. I don't know what the hell he had to be cheerful about, but it was pleasant.

I went on unpacking while he carried the coatrack into the other room and set it next to the boy's bed. I had him plug in the hotplate at the outlet under the boarded window and clear a table for it. We covered the table with a clean towel and lay out things we'd need for general care. It was Pinky's idea to use a double-shot whiskey glass to hold the thermometer. No probationer was ever more zealous. I told him so and promised him his cap if we pulled this one through.

Pinky followed my every move as I hung the plasma flask to the coatrack and held the patient's arm while I found a vein. Afterward, as we sat, Pinky said, "Funny thing about blood, isn't it! When you need it, it doesn't make a hell of a lot of difference whose you get . . . so long as you get it."

"That's right. At least it hasn't made much difference since the general use of plasma."

"Take that stuff up there in the bottle. It could have, come from anybody . . . a minister, a crook, a cop . . . anybody . . . maybe all of them together. But right now it's being used on a guy the State doesn't want in its society. But it'll do him as much good as if he hadn't ever gotten into trouble at all."

I made some crack about science being impersonal.

Pinky sat, thoughtful, a while. "Yeah. I could fill up my car at the police service station and it would run just as well."

I told him I'd advise against it at the moment and he came out with a good healthy chuckle. When I told him we were finished he stood on one foot, then the other, until I'd straightened up the stuff. As we turned off the ceiling light and went into my room again Pinky dug into his pocket and handed me a letter. Before he let go of it, he said, "Your Miss Storm's all right. Read what it says on the envelope. She'd left it out of sight, but where we'd see it before you."

I looked at the familiar long envelope. On the outside she had neatly typed:

> This letter is to Dr. Connor. It is strictly personal in nature and contains nothing which might affect the people with whom he is working. You may read it if you feel it is necessary, but, under any circumstances, please deliver it to the doctor.
>
> K.S.

The seal was unbroken. Pinky was grinning and I spluttered out some sort of appreciation as he left the room with, "Call me when you want your dinner." I turned on the bedside light and lay down for the first time since I had been roused that morning. I opened the letter and read:

Dearest:

I don't know where you are or what you are doing but I am obeying your instructions implicitly. Possibly I'm wrong in doing so, despite the fact that you were so positive over the phone. I believe if you hadn't said you were caring for somebody terribly sick, I'd have disobeyed you. You know, Jimmy, darling, I think you're an awful lug and not to be trusted in the ordinary circumstances of life. But with a really sick patient, I'd trust you beyond belief. Oh, darling, I hope you're not in terrible trouble of some sort!

Well, hell. If you're not in trouble where you are, you're in plenty around here. I've had call after call from your gymnasium pal with whom you had a date at nine this morning. I've simply told him if he can't keep track of you, how can he expect me to. He didn't like it and was very fresh.

Please stop this damned foolishness and come home. I disapprove of you very heartily practically everywhere, but I'd be a lot more comfortable disapproving of you where I can find you once in a while. Please, darling, be careful. For the moment, at least, I send you a lot more love than you deserve.

                                        Katie

P.S. I hope you got the toothbrush.
P.P.S. I don't know anything about your patient, but it sounds like the first serious job you've undertaken since I've known you. Get him well!

I looked in at the kid before I read the letter again. His color was much improved.

13

A shower did me a lot of good and I found I was hungry for the first time. I rang for Pinky and told him so. He asked me if he could have his dinner in my room and I said "Why not?" We settled on steak and he went back down. I took a look at my patient and his heart sounded as though it was taking a bit more interest in its practically hopeless job. His respiration was definitely eased. He was trying to grope his way into consciousness, but would give it up and relax when I spoke gently to him.

I must get a name for this kid.

Pinky was clumping around outside the door and someone was helping him haul the trays up. Finally one pair of feet bumped down the stairs and Pinky hollered, "Hey, Doc! Open the door." I did and a huge tray led the guy in by the arms. It smelled good and we set it on the bed while we cleared a table. They'd even sent a tablecloth so we made something of an occasion of it.

Feet on the stairs again and Pinky went to the door, opened it a crack, reached through and pulled back a bottle of wine. It turned out to be claret and good. We sat down and ate. Pinky's table manners were relaxed and suggested better than ordinary home background. He chatted pleasantly and easily, like a guy lunching at Lindy's. We talked about sports, mostly . . . nice, standard subjects like why there weren't any good English boxers and how good was Primo Carnera. It was all very social and jolly, but neither of us brought up the subjects which were uppermost in our minds.

Pinky rang the bell and pretty soon more feet on the steps and Pinky said, "That'll be coffee. I told them to bring it when I rang." As he took the tray, I heard him say, "When I ring again we'll be in the kid's room. Clear away." I wondered, vaguely, what the relationship was between the front of the house and the back. I asked Pinky.

"They mind their own business out there. There have always been people around on this side of the building and they've learned not to pay too much attention to it." Pinky busied himself with the coffee. "Cream and sugar, Doc?" I told him no and went out to the boy. As I sponged his hot hands and face, he said, "Hey!" His eyes opened all the way for a second and I told him it wasn't time to wake up yet and to go back to sleep. He said, "Water! Jeez, water!" I wet his mouth and let him swallow a little. He lay back and closed his eyes again. As I turned away from the bed, Pinky was standing in the doorway. "I heard him speak."

"Yes. Not a very brilliant conversation but a perfectly normal one. He asked for water. I gave him a little. He'll get a good drink later . . . the sort that won't have to roll around in that hurt belly of his."

"Is he better?"

"I don't know. He looks better. He's still got a gutfull of death. Whether there's enough of him left to take care of it is anybody's guess. We can help him some from here . . . cool him off, nourish his body without taxing his stomach and injured bowel, brace up his heart a little and keep him from suffering too much. That's about all."

We sat quietly for a while. Finally I said, "What do I call the kid?"

"What do you mean . . . call him?"

"I mean what's his name?"

"Come, now, Doctor! Names!"

"Nicknames . . . what do I call the guy?"

"That interests me. Why should you have to have a name for him?"

"For the same reason I have to have a thermometer. It's part of my trade. Patients have to have names . . . especially the very sick ones. Handles you can get hold of them by."

"I'll be damned. Why?"

Great! Education I must give the guy now! "Look, fella, I'm all in and we've got a long job ahead of us . . . tonight, tomorrow night, and more nights. Don't make me give lectures in Psych 4 on top of it. Patients just have to have names . . . I mean the kind they answer to, not something you just make up."

"Okay, Doc, I'll think about it. What say we move into the kid's room a few minutes and let one of the guys clean up this wreckage?"

He rang the bell and we went into the other room.

Pinky closed the bathroom door behind him. The Boy opened his eyes as I put my hand on his head. He said, "Hello," and shut them again. Pinky said, "Hello, kid. How are you feeling?" The boy rolled his eyes. Pinky said, "It's me. You're all right, now. Don't talk. Just rest. You'll be all right." The boy said, "Water!"

I got some ice from the water-pitcher we'd had at dinner and wrapped it in gauze for him to suck and left Pinky to hold it for him while I set up the intravenous glucose flask on the clothes-tree. The boy was moving his arms quite a lot but hadn't done much with his feet so I looked for a vein near his ankle and found a good one.

I taped the needle on and sat at the foot of the bed with my hand on the kid's ankle. Pinky watched the flask, fascinated.

"He's drinking that?"

"Yes. And eating it . . . pretty fair meal at that if you're not a slave to the knife and fork."

"My God!" Pinky sniffed and got up. Somebody was rattling dishes back in my room and Pinky walked through to say something to him. There was some mumbled discussion and Pinky strolled in again. "That stop him from being thirsty in his mouth?"

"Can't you see?"

"What?"

"Watch him run his tongue around his mouth and wet his lips."

"Yeah!" The big guy looked funny as he lolled his own tongue around. "He's getting it, isn't he! Hey, that's all right!" I watched him and wondered what intensity of feeling for the lad on the bed could be responsible for his almost childish happiness as he saw that burning thirst quenched drop by drop.

When we took down the flask Pinky said, "How'll we work the shifts tonight. It's ten o'clock."

"How about four hours on and four off until we each get a little rest? I'll be needed this first four. Suppose you grab some sleep and turn up about three?"

"Suits me." He sank down further in his chair and showed no signs of leaving. "Say, Doc."

"What?"

"You called me 'Pinky' this morning. Why?"

"You object to it?"

"I spent a lot of years fighting over it as a kid, but it stuck. Let's not fence. You can't afford to and I don't know how." Not unpleasantly, but it wasn't any tea-party. "Why the 'Pinky'?"

"It was apparently unwise."

"I'll say it was. Where did you get the name?"

"Actually, it was nothing more than a hunch."

"Let's not kid around, Doc. You would have said 'Red.'"

"I don't mean just an idea. I mean it is based on nothing more than a word spoken to me by a person who doesn't know who you are, plus a guess after I'd seen the color of your hair."

"Only that much?"

"Only that much." Then, as an afterthought. "I don't know any more about you now then I did then."

"And who was the person who mentioned my name?"

I pondered this over. There wasn't much to lose or win by not telling. Terry Hale wasn't apt to get hurt, what with the police escort she probably had if she were out of jail.

"I don't know why I shouldn't tell you because the person knew absolutely nothing about you, who you were or what you might, possibly, have to do with her affairs. It was Terry Hale."

Pinky was startled. "But that can't be! Terry Hale! Harry Lennen's girl!" I told him that was right and decided to hang on to as much of the story as I could, using the Hale conversation as the basis for my whole interest in the affair . . . if I was supposed to have any. "Terry Hale! How did it come up, Doc?"

"Terry came to me the other night, scared to death, and told me somebody had killed Harry Lennen and that the police had dragged her in immediately for questioning. Lennen had owed her some money . . ."

"What's that got to do with me? What did she say about me?"

"Actually nothing. This is the way it was. Lennen had called her the night he was killed and asked her to meet him at his apartment. She was jealous and was curious as to where Lennen was when he called. While he was talking, she heard somebody holler something about 'Pinky' and she mentioned it to me. That's all."

"Did she consider it important? Is that why she told you?"

"I doubt it. She didn't know any 'Pinky' and let it go at that."

"So it was Terry Hale who got you interested in Harry Lennen's death. It could have been that way, of course. I hadn't thought of it." He got up and walked toward the bathroom. I sensed his relief. "Yes, it could have been that way."

I followed him into the other room. The dinner litter had been neatly straightened up. Pinky picked up the Forester bottle and held it to the light, put it down without comment. "That Terry Hale story takes a little of the pressure off, Doc, if it's true . . . pressure off you. I'm glad."

"We don't have to be heavy-handed then?"

"I don't. You can be as tough as you like." He laughed. "See you at two-thirty or three?"

"Right . . . no hurry."

He'd reached the hall and had started to close the door when he stuck his head in and said, "Why does a patient have to have a name?"

I burned . . . not unpleasantly. You can do that, you know. I said, "Goddammit, because when they start drifting off from you, you've got something to pull them back with!"

"Now there's something! That . . ."

"I know. That interests you. Listen! When you get really up against it in this doctoring business . . . when you get a guy with a bellyful of bullets and pus . . . he's doing his damnedest to die and get it over with and you're doing your damnedest to keep him from doing it. You're in sort of a contest with God."

"God?"

"God or Providence or Nature . . . or something like that. Whoever . . . or whatever . . . it is that pulls your patient toward, the other side . . . away from life."

"Tug-of-war." Pinky grinned.

"It's a little like trying to find out who owns a dog. You put a dog on a line between two people and each one calls him . . ."

"You and God." Pinky laughed.

I really burned. "Listen, goddammit, I simply asked you . . ."

"Call him 'Fargo' . . . he'll answer to that."

Pinky closed the door. Very gently.

14

The boy . . . Fargo . . . was lying quietly. He was conscious but too sick to care much now that he wasn't so thirsty. I think he was probably sufficiently conscious to realize that I was a stranger and that he shouldn't do any talking. One thing sure, he wasn't well enough to be interested in anything but living. I went into his room and fooled around with one eye on him. He was making little circles with the thumb and fingers of his right hand . . . one after the other. I got the stuff ready to clean him up a little and change the pads over his drains. When I came within range of his vision he watched me through partially opened eyes. When I moved about the room he made no attempt to turn his head. Even when I turned the covers back, he didn't try to look down at his belly. He watched me.

When I'd finished with his bandage I swabbed him down as best I could with alcohol. His body was hard; stringy and knotty; without fat. I decided he might be older than I first thought . . . maybe twenty-three or four. His face looked younger than his body. He had a button nose and dark curly hair. The face of a choirboy and the body of a featherweight fighter . . . or a slightly oversize jockey. Whatever his age and whatever his trade, he wasn't the sort of kid I'd pick to be mixed up in a gun battle and a murder.

Let's see, now. I didn't think Terry Hale was the sort to be mixed up in a murder, either. Nor Sam Eckman. Nor Pinky. As far as Jocko Burns went, I had appointed myself his personal representative and protector. Good old Doc! And they thought William Jennings Bryan was the great humanitarian!

As I wound up my ministrations to Fargo, I swung the bed-lamp aside and said, "Anything else you want, kid?" He opened his eyes slowly and seemed to be making an effort to think. He looked at me with that directness you see so often in the sick . . . people who, otherwise, might be shy. After a while he said, "Pinky," very distinctly. I told him Pinky was asleep but would be up and stay with him later. "I'm the doctor," I told him. "How do you feel?"

"Okay, I guess." I didn't argue with him. His eyes told me he wanted to say something else and was debating it. I waited. In a moment he said, "Doc."

"Yes?"

"How bad am I hurt?"

"Pretty badly. You got hit in sort of a mean spot."

He thought this over, then he said, "I had an operation."

"That's right. I did it. That's why I'm here."

"You're Doc Connor."

"Right again."

"I heard about you."

"You did, eh? Where?" The boy grinned a little.

"Around." He sighed and moved as if to turn away, made a little grimace of pain and settled down again. I said, "Okay, you've talked enough for now. I'll see you later. I'm right in the next room so speak your piece if you want anything."

"Thanks." I started for the door. "Say, Doc."

"What?"

"What are my chances? I know they ain't good."

"I'll tell you, Fargo . . ." He looked a little startled until I told how I got his name. "I'll tell you. A few hours ago I wouldn't have gambled a dime on your chances. Right now you look like a champion. I think you're going to be all right, but I'll have to have a lot of help from you. Are you game?"

"Nobody ever said I wasn't, Doc. Thanks."

I went back to my room.

Somebody downstairs was having a steak . . . apparently well done. The smoke frying odor was drifting in strongly. I noticed, idly, that it didn't seem to be coming up the stairway as I had thought, but from someplace overhead. For want of something more profitable to do, I prowled around trying to trace it. There was no opening from which it could come in my room and the windows were as tightly sealed as a workmanlike carpentering job could make them.

I sniffed around in Fargo's room, quietly, with the same result but, in passing through the bathroom on the way back, I found it . . . a grilled ventilator apparently intended to circulate the air in the place. The kitchen sounds, and a lot of others, came up as strongly as the kitchen odors. I climbed up on the tub and listened. Somebody, practically in my ear, said, "Two, well-done . . . take 'em away, Charley!" That would be the steaks. After that I heard an indistinct rumble of men's voices under the kitchen sounds and, for the first time, I heard a cash register.

The geography of the building held a sudden and absorbing interest for me. The orchestra seemed less distinct through the ventilator than in my room. I guessed the kitchen must be just, or nearly, below me. I was sure the murmur of men's voices, also, had been from someplace besides the main club room.

The office where I had telephoned Katie had been definitely in the direction of this . . . our . . . side of the house. With the rough conception I had formed of the first floor, that room, the office, could have been next to the kitchen. It would adjoin the main club room, as it conveniently might for business reasons, and fall partly under my room and partly under Fargo's, including, of course, the bathroom.

I waited endlessly for the telephone to ring but didn't hear it. The kitchen sounds were so loud I suppose I wouldn't have heard it anyway. I made up my mind to listen again and climbed down. My ventilator could prove a most valuable source of information when the kitchen wasn't working. Providing, of course, that the thing led to that office.

About two o'clock I took a shower and shaved. The yen for something long and cool overtook me and I gave a short punch on the bell. In a minute or two I heard clumping on the stairs and somebody knocked heavily on the door. I recognized the laryngitic voice of my friend the chauffeur of yesterday morning. "What'll ya have, Doc?"

"See if you can hustle me a big, tall ginger ale and some ice, will you, pal?"

"Sure. Easy." He bumped his way along the corridor and back down the stairs. In a couple of minutes he was back with it, unlocked the door and told me to reach out and get it. He was against the door and hanging onto the knob. The drink was on the floor and he told me to pick it up. I did. He closed the door and the key grated in the lock.

A modicum of the Old Forester put the ginger ale into first class drinking condition. It was about half gone when Fargo tried to move around and hurt himself doing it. He was pretty miserable when I went in.

"Hurt bad, Fargo?"

"It's pretty rough, Doc." He smiled but it was a little wan.

"I'll give you something for it. You need rest, now . . . all you can get. Don't fret any more than you can help . . . and don't think about anything but getting well, see?"

"Yeah. I'll try, Doc."

"Feel up to holding the thermometer in your mouth a while?"

"Sure."

I stuck the thermometer under his tongue while I prepared the hypodermic. At least Pinky wouldn't have much trouble during his shift. The boy's temperature had come down some from its dramatic peaks, but wasn't anything to cheer about. I brought him the duck and swabbed him off with alcohol after I'd given him the hypo. I put the lamp down on the floor and went back to my room.

About a quarter to three Pinky came in looking much refreshed. Somebody behind him locked the door and retreated downstairs. Pinky laughed. "That locks us both in for the night, Doctor. How you holding up?"

I told him I was all right and noted that he looked rested.

"I don't usually need much rest . . . good thing, too. I haven't had much lately." He sat down after glancing into the other room. "Now that you've got a handle to pull your patient with, how's the tug-of-war with God?"

"I damned near scared the kid to death when I called him Fargo. I told him you'd given me his name. He's some better."

"How much better, Doc?"

"I don't know. His temperature is about where you'd expect it with that sort of an infection . . . but down some. He just seems better. He's been talking rationally."

"Talking?" Pinky's voice was too gentle. He probably had wanted to shout.

"Yes. Rationally. He knew what he was saying."

"I see." He lit a cigarette. I decided to make a speech.

"Look here. This boy is in no shape to take any bullying or threatening. He's going to be in a lot of pain before long and he'll have to have sedation . . . morphine. He may talk . . . irrationally. He may talk that way when I'm around and you're not. But I want this understood . . ."

"Hold it, Doc." Pinky walked across the room and rubbed out the new cigarette in the ash tray by the bed. "Take it easy." I held it while he walked back and sat down again. "Nobody's going to bully this kid or threaten him . . . although I know some people who would if they could get their hands on him right now. As you say, he may talk. Rationally or irrationally or any other way. Instead of my wanting you *not* to listen to what he may say, Doc, I want you to remember . . . I want you to write down . . . every word of it."

"Why?"

"Because way back in this kid's mind someplace is the answer to some questions that have to be answered before any of us see daylight again . . . and that includes you, Doc."

"Can you tell me anything more about it? What sort of questions might bring out such an answer?" Pinky shook his head, leaned over and rested his elbows on his knees. He stared at the floor a while.

"No questions. Questions won't work. He's been scared with questions. I can't go any further." The redhead got up again and walked through the bathroom. He stood looking at the sleeping boy, shook his head as if he were trying to rid himself of an ugly memory. When he came back he said, "You'd better get some sleep."

Fargo cried out softly and Pinky hurried into the other room. There were no further sounds but in a minute or two I smelled the rubbing alcohol and I knew I wouldn't have to worry much about the patient's general care in the next four hours.

The day wound itself up in the joint below. A car pulled away. The general clattering in the kitchen died down. Somebody was singing *Only a Shanty in Old Shantytown.*

15

Somebody said, "Good morning," and I woke up. It was almost eight. Pinky was standing in the bathroom door with two towels over his shoulder and the duck in his hand. I sat on the edge of the bed and said:

"Lessee that."

"What?"

"The duck . . . the thing you've got in your hand."

"Good God! Before breakfast?"

"Not by choice. Why'd you let me sleep so long?"

"You looked so pretty I didn't have the heart to wake you." Pinky strolled over with the duck. I made a note to give the kid more fluids and asked Pinky how his patient was.

"I think you'll find him better."

"Was he restless?"

"He hardly moved except in the last hour or so . . . then he was uncomfortable and thirsty. I fixed some ice like you showed me yesterday and he quieted down. His belly hurt him some."

"It'll hurt more." I got up and went to Fargo's room.

Pinky went back to his bathroom duties. I sat down by his bed and the boy said, "Hello, Doc."

"Hello, kid. How do you feel?"

"Pretty lousy, Doc." There was no complaint in it and he smiled when he said it. "My stomach hurts pretty bad sometimes."

Pinky called in from the bathroom, "An hour ago he said he was hungry." The boy said, "Not any more. I guess I just thought I was."

I told him we'd feed him all right, but that the beefsteaks would have to wait. Pinky helped me set up the glucose flask before he went downstairs promising to bring back some breakfast. A shower and one of the borrowed shirts got things under way for the day and, before long, Pinky came in with a handsome breakfast of ham and eggs, a man-sized stack of toast and a huge pot of coffee. There was a morning paper on the tray. It looked pretty well read and I figured, why not? I imagined most of the people, whoever they were, in that house that morning would be thoroughly interested in the morning papers.

We set the time for changing shifts for one-thirty and I listened to Pinky's steps down the stairs and into the kitchen.

I spread out the paper and started to eat. The Lennen story was still fresh enough to be pretty well forward but not important enough to rate much display. It took a respectable hunk of page five. There was a cheese-cake picture of Terry Hale captioned "Taxi Dancer Held for Questioning in Lennen Slaying." I figured there couldn't have been any very important developments because the story was pretty routine. A round-up story of things I'd already known. I think I was a little disappointed that nobody seemed to have observed that I was missing from my usual haunts. I was not completely neglected, however. One paragraph said that "a search is being conducted for certain other persons who are believed to possess information vital to the case."

Another paragraph disturbed me because Eddie Marsh is always conservative in his statements and promises to newspapermen. It read:

> Police Lieutenant Edward Quinn Marsh, in charge of the investigation, has promised important revelations within the next twenty-four hours. Lieutenant Marsh told reporters he was verifying certain facts concerning Terry Hale's past life which he believed would solve the case at once. He added that the verifications required the assistance of out-of-state police, however, and that he was

unable to say just when they would be completed.
Miss Hale, in private life, is Gladys Eckman,
daughter of Sam Eckman, the horse trainer, who
is now racing at local tracks.

Well, well! I knew Eddie wasn't kidding the papers. He's
known as the poorest source of news in the Department. You
could pretty well bank on the fact that he'd turn up some dirt on
La Belle Hale. You could also bank on the fact that it wouldn't
be trivial scandal. It would have a direct bearing on the Lennen
murder. I finished up my breakfast with a lot of stuff on my
mind . . . a lot of vague, apparently unrelated facts which added
up to exactly nothing.

The kitchen sounds had rattled themselves out and Fargo
was quietly staring at the diminishing level of his glucose bottle. I heard a single voice downstairs. It sounded like Pinky and
I decided to try listening at the ventilator. At Fargo's bathroom
door I said, "I'll shut this a minute if you don't mind." He said,
"Sure, Doc. I'm modest myself." I shut the door and climbed up
on the tub. It was Pinky all right and he was at the telephone.
I'd missed the number business because all he said to the operator was, "That's right." There was some delay before he got his
connection.

"Good morning." After this there was a long pause. It could
have been a lengthy, prearranged report. Pinky snapped, "That's
a guess." His voice was suddenly harsh, defensive. "Get that out
of your head." The words weren't loud but they cracked like
a whiplash . . . a Pinky I hadn't known before . . . a Pinky I
shouldn't care to face in a row. "You've got all the testimony in
front of you. For God's sake use your head, man!" Apparently
the other fellow made some protest to this. There was a brief
pause before Pinky went on. "Listen. I've been studying that
document for seven years. There was somebody else. A man.
A man here in New York. The only person who knew who he
was is dead. But there's some connection between that man and
Kerschoff. Find it."

During the pause I kept thinking of the name Kerschoff. Something nibbled at my memory yet evaded me. Kerschoff. Kerschoff.

"No. It doesn't make any difference where we are. You're better off not knowing. I'll call you not later than nine tomorrow morning. If anything breaks I'll know about it and call you. When you hear anything, get back to base. Right? Okay. Bye."

I climbed down from the bathtub wondering about somebody by the name of Kerschoff.

I put away the intravenous equipment, took the kid's temperature . . . it was improved . . . and went to work at changing the dressing. I heard Pinky's step on the stairs but didn't look up as he came in. He paused in the other room, then I sensed him standing back of me, watching. He made a sound of disgust and said, "Lord, what a mess!" As I glanced over my shoulder, he looked pretty worn.

"Why don't you get some rest?"

He sighed unconsciously and started to turn away. "I'm headed for bed right now. Thought you might have a favorite radio program you'd like to listen to . . . a thriller, maybe."

"If you think I haven't you're crazy . . ."

"I left the portable in the other room."

"That's wonderful . . . thanks. I'll certainly use it." There wasn't any reason why the guy should bother with a radio for me . . . as a matter of fact, there might be a pretty good reason why he shouldn't. I didn't think much about how it could be, but there might be some danger to Pinky in even a one-sided contact with the outside. As he left the room he turned back with a big grin. "If you hear any specially helpful household hints, let me know."

I followed his steps until they faded out in some far part of the house below.

Fargo lay still, watching me, until I'd finished with him. I'd have given a lot to know what was going on in his mind. I had an idea that, between us, we had enough knowledge to convict somebody. It was not a comforting thought for a man who found himself in the position of hostage . . . prisoner of the person the information would possibly, if not probably, convict. My host's geniality need be nothing more than an intelligent man's way of making the best of an unpleasant situation. It would be a bad mistake to sell Pinky short as a tough guy until such time as he had some reason to be tough. He had been tough enough the morning he brought me here. On the telephone he had sounded more than tough. His voice had been vicious.

Yes. Whatever information I had, I decided to keep for safer circumstances. If I had had any doubts about it, they were dispelled shortly afterward. It was that afternoon I got my first warning from Katie.

The radio worked pretty well and I got some sort of an idea of locating myself by the intensities of the stations as they came in but gave it up. The only source of activity I could locate positively was the refrigerator downstairs.

A news program said nothing whatever about the Lennen murder as I tried to kill time over lunch. Katie's familiar theme found me in front of the portable waiting for those damned recipes like a kid at a circus.

Then Katie. Oh brotherrr! Did you ever hear a lute or something across the moonlit waters of Lake Como? It must be like Katie's little song of welcome to her radio audience. She sounds exactly like she is . . . beautiful, intelligent, assured. I had a fleeting resentment that she could be so calm and gay while I was listening to her 'way off here . . . practically in a dungeon. I had a look at the Forester and voted against it in view of a pamphlet I once read about resentments and alcoholism.

Katie introduced her guest-of-the-day, a guy who had spent three years among the pygmies and apparently had written a book which he cared to have people buy. She described him in a rather odious way, I thought, which made him sound like a cross between Tyrone Power and Buffalo Bill. It was her custom to introduce the guests at the opening of her show and then let them hang fire until she got through with her commercials. Her announcer was supposed to intersperse a smart crack or so . . .

something of an intimate nature which allegedly gave a warm feeling to the program. The fellow has always seemed somewhat soupy to me.

She had some dandy hints to offer which I imagine would be extremely helpful to people who need hints. She also gave out with a way to give charm and dignity to a New England boiled dinner. It had something to do with the color scheme and stuff to put in the juice.

Then, suddenly, it was unKatie and unfamiliar. The gal gets a tremendous mail response from her program and has a secretary to help her answer it . . . but she never talks about it on the air. She said . . .

"Thanks for your many letters and cards. I'm always happy to hear from you all. This morning's mail brought a note from one of my young friends, Eddie M., who wants me to send a personal message to his shut-in pal, Jimmy. He says they won't let Jimmy come out of the house to play and, as Eddie describes it, 'It ain't healthy.' Okay, Eddie, we hope Jimmy will be hearing this and get out again as soon as he can. We certainly don't want him to stay anyplace where it ain't healthy for him!

"So much for the mail . . . now let's see if we have any other business to take up before we get back to Dr. Hutchison and the pygmies . . ."

Eddie Marsh must have turned on the heat. Naturally, since I had so completely disappeared without even calling Katie . . . to his knowledge . . . his best guess was that somebody had me. He had always thought I knew more than I actually did about the case, anyway. So he was telling me it was "unhealthy." Marsh is not a guy to be easily stampeded . . . and certainly not one to ring Katie in on it unless it was pretty urgent.

A moment after I'd shut off the radio I heard the phone downstairs and hurried to the ventilator. It was almost time for Pinky to come up so I locked both bathroom doors. It was his voice down the shaft, however.

". . . yes . . . yes . . . certainly I heard it. . . . Look, chappie, you take care of your end and I'll take care of mine. If there are any radio programs that need listening to, I'll do it from here.

. . . Of course! Of course! You think I think it's funny? . . . Sure it may be a shot in the dark, but I'm the guy that's getting shot at and I'll make damned sure the next one doesn't come any closer. Keep after the Kerschoff tie-up and don't get far away from your phone." He hung up and I climbed down and went back into my room with the little bell ringing insistently in the back of my head. This time I'd better listen. If it wasn't too late to listen to the bell . . . or Eddie . . . or anybody.

Pinky's step sounded formidable on the stairs. I kept trying to drive his telephone conversation out of my head and revert to the way I'd be if I'd just heard the radio program and nothing more. The door opened and the fellow walked in without a greeting. There didn't seem to be any necessity for saying anything. He sat down and lit a cigarette. After a few long seconds he looked up.

"Any helpful household hints, Doc?" It would have been more comfortable if he'd smiled, but it was definitely my turn to talk.

"I took it for granted you heard the program. I would have told you if you hadn't seemed so serious." I was telling him the truth and felt like it sounded that way. It had damned well better!

"Yes. I heard it. The girl has talked, of course." There was no suggestion of a question in his voice. It was a flat statement.

"No." It would be difficult to convince him of that yet. I would have staked my life on the fact that she hadn't. Come to think of it, that's probably what I was staking.

"Yes. It has to be that way. She said 'won't let him come out of the house.' She has to have told Marsh." He wasn't arguing. He simply brushed off my statement.

I went on, "Eddie Marsh had told me to be at his office at nine o'clock yesterday . . . good God, was it only yesterday? I wasn't there. I was here. Katie started to say over the phone yesterday . . . you must have heard her . . . she started to say that Marsh had been calling her."

"I supposed that was what she meant. Yes, I heard her." He stared at the floor. "That means nothing."

"Then you definitely heard her say Marsh had been calling her. You say that means nothing. I say that means nothing too. She's the first person . . . the only person as far as that goes . . . that Marsh would call. He had every reason to believe I'd got myself into some trouble. He thought I knew more about the Lennen business than I'd admitted to him."

"Do you?" He looked up with a bit of a twisted grin on his face that was not reassuring.

"Hell no. I haven't the slightest idea of any of it . . . why Lennen was killed . . . how a guy like that could have ten grand on him . . . I don't even know who he was. Marsh says his name wasn't Lennen."

"Did you read the paper this morning?"

"The Lennen story? Yes, I read it. There wasn't much in it."

Pinky looked very serious. He got up and walked across the room. He picked up the paper and threw it down again. "There was a hell of a lot in it, Doc. A hell of a lot. When your friend Marsh finishes what he calls his 'out-of-state verifications' on Terry Hale, it's only a question of time until we'll have to move. Your girl friend's talking just makes it sure. Don't bother to argue. I can't afford to believe you. From here in, Doc, the chips are down. I'm sorry. I'd hoped we could do it the nice way."

16

The chill was on.

A strained, distrustful courtesy seemed to be the order of the day and it was damned uncomfortable. There was no question about the fact that Pinky was worried. When I'd given him his instructions for Fargo's care during his shift he closed the boy's door and followed me into my room.

"How soon can this kid be moved?"

"He can't . . . if you mean within the next week or two." Though I felt fairly confident the boy would recover, I didn't see any reason why I should offer aid and comfort to the enemy. "Just because he quit dying for twenty-four hours is no sign he's getting well. I take it for granted you hadn't thought of moving him in an ambulance."

He gave me a fast look, opened his mouth and closed it again. I took off my clothes and put on my borrowed pajamas. At the moment, nothing seemed to make much difference to me except my bed. Recovery from that bone-deep fatigue rated top priority in my book. I'd need the rest plenty before long. If I had to pick a spot for a guy who couldn't hold his eyes open, I wouldn't pick this one. As I climbed in, Pinky came out of Fargo's room and closed the door.

"You better get all the sleep you can, Doc, you may have to work a double shift tonight." Then he disappeared again, closing the door on my side of the bathroom as he went back to stand his watch. I pondered a while on the nature of his errand. He must have meant to leave the place because nothing short of

a load of cops would have made him miss his nursing job while
he was in the house. I hadn't heard any telephone conversation
during which arrangements had been made for tonight's possible excursion and figured there would be one sooner or later.
While I was resolving to cat-nap with one eye on Pinky and one
ear on the telephone, I corked off.

Vague dream problems beset me as I slept the violent sleep
of exhaustion . . . living the disturbed, inverted after-images
of regeneration. Once I think I was wakened by the juke-box.
Another time I had the sharp impression of a car roaring away
from the place with a hoarse shout on its tail. Then Pinky was
standing by the bed and there was a tray on the table. He stated
his business, leaving out the amenities.

"You'd better take over now. I'm needed downstairs. There's
some food on the table. The kid needs you, too. He's in considerable pain."

Just that. No more. I said thanks and he was gone. He was
neither surly nor courteous. He was busy. I decided to let my
dinner sit while I fooled around in the bathroom and kept my ear
toward the ventilator. Fargo was pretty miserable as his torn and
manhandled bowel began protesting its treatment. Katie's supplies
had included a tube and I set about giving the boy some relief.

When I went back to my tray it was eight-thirty and the
food was cold. People had come in downstairs and the juke-box
was blasting. Kitchen noises had already made my ventilator
useless and I gave up the idea of trying to find out anything
about Pinky's expedition. Cars came and left but none seemed
to come from the back side of the house where I knew Pinky's
car was kept. I ate some of the coldish food without enthusiasm.

Pinky had left the portable radio. I hadn't thought about
it before, but I should have expected him to take it away from
me. I suppose he figured that I couldn't do any further damage
no matter what I heard. He'd see to that personally. I got the
nine o'clock news. It was strictly national in scope and didn't
include any mention of the Lennen affair.

About midnight I shut off the radio. Fargo, in his room, had
fallen asleep listening to a soothing disc-jockey, who alternated

quiet recordings with sedative poetry. Business downstairs was apparently dull because there was almost no customer noise and the slot machine sounded the only business transactions as it grabbed an occasional quarter from the musicians. I took a shower and decided to flap around in my pajamas.

Once, during the next hour I heard the telephone ring. Very distinctly. I crawled up to my battle-station but couldn't make out whose voice it was or anything that was said. Before I left the ventilator, however, I did hear someone say, "Oscar! Go out on the porch and turn off the sign. The boss says it's quiet enough to close early." It had been quiet last night, too, but they hadn't closed.

There was no doubt of the fact that things were starting to happen around our little castle and, as the occupant of the tower-room, I wasn't too happy about it. The situation had lost plenty of glamour as far as I was concerned and I wasn't crazy about the look of the immediate future. For curiosity I tried the handle of my door . . . with fast and positive results. A voice rasped, "Want somepin', Doc?"

I said, "No. I was wondering if I was still locked in."

"You're locked in all right," he leaned close to the crack in the door and I observed that he was a gin drinker. "What'd you do to the boss, anyway?" Pal to pal, this was.

"I didn't do anything to him. Why?"

"'ause you ain't only locked in, mister, but I got to stay out here in the hall all night. So don't start nothing." Hell of a time to start anything. I tried to laugh it off.

"Must be lonesome out there. Come in and have a drink. We'll play some two-handed stud."

"Are you kiddin'?" The big lug said nothing more and I heard his clumsy step down the hall. He grunted and sat down on what I suppose was the top step. My fleeting thought of escape was settled at least for the night.

When I came back to Fargo's room he was awake again and making thoughtful circles with his fingers. He said he felt some better but wasn't very sleepy. He evidently had something on his mind and I pulled the big chair around where I could half face him. For the first time since I'd been with him, he asked me if he could have a cigarette. I lighted one for him and found an ash tray on the bureau. We both smoked for a while in silence. He watched me covertly with the friendly and appealing shyness you find so often in boys and miss so often in their elders. I waited him out.

"Doc . . ." he hesitated as though he were searching for unfamiliar words. "You ain't here because you want to be . . . are you?" Once he'd got it out, his gaze was direct and frank.

"No, Fargo, I'm not." There wasn't any percentage in inventing something to tell him when he probably knew, or could easily guess, the truth. "But now that I'm here, I want to see you through all this."

"Pinky made you come here to take care of me." I told him that was right and he went on. "But you haven't tried to get away because I need doctoring."

"Something like that. Of course I gave quite a lot of thought to the fact that somebody'd probably shoot me if I tried to get away." At that, I was making myself look too good. A mental image of old laryngitis out in the hall proved the point.

"But you don't stop to figure out whether I'm a bad guy and ain't worth saving or not. You just go ahead and fix me up . . . even if you turn me in to the cops later. Why is that?"

"I guess it's because, when a fella's got a bullet-hole in his belly, everybody including the law calls time out until the doctor gets through with him. Bad guys and good guys look pretty much alike on the inside."

"Yeah. That's what I mean. They all have to take time out until the doctor gets through. Doctors are special. They know more about you than you do, yourself. You can't use the same rules on doctors that you do on other people."

"That's a dangerous philosophy, kid. Better try to get to sleep." He didn't say anything more and I went back to my room. The sounds below had faded out. There were occasional noises of closing up and some two or three cars drove off. I was listening to a late local program when I heard a car drive into the garage at the back of the house. That would be Pinky coming home from his trip. He came in the back door, slamming it after him, and spoke to somebody in the kitchen. It was only a few minutes later that I heard him climbing the stairs. I turned off the radio and waited. He unlocked and opened the door and came in.

"Hello, Doc." You couldn't tell anything about his mood from his voice or his face. I said hello and waited some more. "Hear anything more on the radio?" I told him I hadn't and he said, "You will." While he stared at the floor he asked me how Fargo was. I told him. He got up and walked through and spoke to the boy. As he came back he closed both bathroom doors and stood in front of my chair.

"Doc, I was out tonight and I talked to my attorney. Something has been bothering me and I found out what to do about it. It concerns you."

"Me?" I had a passing thought that he'd asked his lawyer how much more trouble he'd be in if he knocked me off!

"Yes." I started to get up. He motioned to me and sat down himself. "I don't suppose it has occurred to you to wonder why I haven't asked you for the slug you took out of Fargo, has it?"

"The slug I took out of Fargo?" It was silly of me to say it, of course.

"Let's be adult, Doc. I'm worn out. I can't play games tonight."

"Okay, then. It hasn't occurred to me. Why haven't you?"

"Because I had a hunch that I shouldn't have anything to do with that slug . . . that I should never touch it. So I didn't. Tonight I found out I was right . . . and why. Nobody has touched that piece of lead since you found it in the kid's gut . . . right?"

"That's right. I found it completely by accident. In this sort of a case you don't go messing around looking for things like that."

"But you found it. You hid it. Then you retrieved it from that nasty mess somewhere before you left the operating room. Right?"

"Right." It began to dawn on me what he was driving at.

"If you had to swear to that in court, would you?"

"Of course. If it's never been out of my possession, I'll certainly know it's the slug that injured the boy. But how would it get into court . . . that is to say . . . without your . . ."

"Without my facing a kidnaping charge?" The guy stared at the floor again. "I'm afraid it wouldn't. That's why I'll do everything within my power to prevent that slug from turning up in your hand in a courtroom . . . but, if it does, I want to know that you would identify it."

"I see."

"I wish to hell you did see sometimes, Doc, but I can't gamble on you. The way this hand plays, I can't gamble on anybody . . . even this stupid mouthpiece of mine who told me what to do with the slug. It looks wrong to me but I haven't any choice."

I said, "What do you . . . or rather, what does your attorney want me to do with the slug?"

"He says for me not to go near it. Not to touch it. He also says for me not to leave it with you any longer for fear there might be some . . . misunderstanding." Pinky didn't grin as he might have yesterday. He scowled . . . more, I believe, in puzzlement than in anger. "You are to send it to Eddie Marsh."

I was completely confused. "In your position, that doesn't make any sense!" Pinky sat absolutely still and suddenly I had an extremely nasty thought. I had to express it out loud. "You have just finished telling me that you'd do everything in your power to keep that slug and me from getting together in a courtroom. Now you send the thing to Eddie Marsh . . . practically *insuring* its presence in that courtroom . . ."

Pinky interrupted. ". . . and, to subtract one of my statements from the other, I have simply said, in substance, that I shall do everything in my power to keep you out of the courtroom." Pinky did grin that time and I wasn't having any. I didn't like any part of that grin. He was instantly serious again, his eyes directly on mine. "It *may* not be as bad as it sounds. It can be worse. I can't tell you any more about it. But I can tell you that you will have no choice about sending the slug to Marsh."

"What if I tell you I threw it away?"

"You won't. Let's not start playing games again." Reaching into his breast pocket, he pulled out a big envelope and handed it to me. "Here's the note. It's inside the envelope. I haven't touched it. It's on dime store paper and pronounced untraceable by experts. All it needs is for you to press the slug into the cardboard arrangement you'll find inside, sign the note, seal it up, put it back in this big envelope and we'll do the rest."

"You can't tell me anything more?"

"I could tell you a lot of things, Doc." He got up and walked around as though he, too, were looking for some way out of the room. "I could tell you a lot of things . . . and every damned one of them would make you a worse threat to my . . . call it freedom. Your problem is bad enough as it is." He turned back to me. "That slug may be the only thing in existence which will keep you *out* of that courtroom . . . and as for me . . ." He shrugged; stretched and closed his big hands. "Read the note and sign it. I don't want to talk any more."

I opened the big envelope and took out a smaller one, a sort of package with a thick double cardboard filler. The top layer of cardboard had a hole cut into it. The hole was almost exactly the right size. I looked up at Pinky. "Somebody knew the caliber of the slug all right." He said, "Yes, we knew." I read the note:

> Lieut. Edward Marsh,
>   Police Headquarters,
>   New York City.
> Dear Eddie:
> The enclosed bullet is sent to you for safekeeping. It is sealed in the cardboard container which bears my signature. If you open it, please do so in the presence of witnesses.
>   The police do not know by whom it was fired, from what weapon, nor whom it struck. It is not sought in evidence in connection with any act of violence now known to you or to the police of any other city.

I can only impress upon you that it is important both to you and to me and that I shall be able to identify it when and if it becomes necessary. It will be to our mutual advantage to avoid making this matter public until later.

Sincerely yours,

James C. Connor, M.D.

When I'd finished reading, Pinky said, "It's very important to me, Doc. Shall we have it the nice way?"

I stuck my hand in my pocket and hauled out the slug.

When all the details were accomplished and the package slipped back into the large envelope without Pinky's touching it, he said, "Thanks, Doc. It had to be this way." He went out, locked the door and walked rather quickly down the stairs. In a moment I heard the familiar clodhoppers of my guard. In another minute or two I heard a car go out the back and I knew that my only hold on Pinky was on its way to Eddie Marsh through some busy midtown post-office.

17

It had been a knock at the door that awakened me that third day and I had watched Pinky answer it to haul in my tray. He put the lunch on the table and, for the first time, looked over at me.

"Oh. You're awake. Here's some food." I thanked him and went about the business of getting up. Quite casually he said, "The morning paper's there, too. You'll find quite a lot of news in it." I said, "Oh?" He stood there a moment watching me. When he spoke it was with considerable and visible restraint. "Your friend Eddie Marsh has decided to say things."

"About me?"

"No. He's holding the umbrella over you like a good pal. But he's still a cop and, from what I hear, he's not the kind of guy to cover up for anyone too long." Pinky went into Fargo's room and came out with a necktie which he stuffed in his pocket. "The story's about Terry Hale. It will be news to you." With that he dismissed the subject and went into his report about the patient's morning. The boy was apparently much improved.

I forced myself to eat some breakfast and get finished with Fargo before I picked up the paper. My first glance told me that Pinky had been right . . . Eddie Marsh had decided to say things.

DANCER DISCLOSED AS LENNEN'S WIFE
TERRY HALE ADMITS
MARRIAGE TO MURDER VICTIM
After persistently denying any more than a casual

friendship with Harry Lennen, found murdered
in his Fifty-third Street apartment Monday night,
Terry Hale, taxi-dancer, has admitted she married
Lennen in 1936.

Oh brother! If I had had any reason to doubt what a lousy
detective I was, it was all there for me to see. Right on the line.

Investigators under the direction of Police Lieutenant Edward Marsh uncovered the record of the
marriage at Warrenton, Va., where the couple is
said to have lived for a time. The woman had giv-
en her right name, Gladys Eckman, and Lennen
had given his name as Frank Parrish.

Frank Parrish . . . Harry Lennen. The name Frank Parrish
was, for some reason, familiar to me. I groped a while but
couldn't get anything. There were a lot of years in there between that wouldn't let me find it.

Further investigation disclosed that Parrish had
been known as an amateur steeplechase jockey
who had ridden with some success in the hunt
meetings throughout Virginia and the Carolinas.

That was it, of course. I'd never known a lot about the guy,
but those were the years when I'd still been doing a little amateur jump riding myself in the summers and followed the hunt
meeting news religiously. The formal "Mr. Parrish" which must
have appeared on racing programs seemed incongruous as hell
against my picture of Harry Lennen.

Maybe not, though. Any old horseman will tell you that
the nicest people in the world . . . and the nastiest . . . are
to be found around horses. Runners, jumpers, trotters and
show-horses alike attract people whose sincere love of the sport
is beyond any sort of cheapness. They also attract people whose

love of money is equally sincere and, therefore, people who are thoroughly contemptible.

Most of these, as you find them around professional race-courses, are pretty well recognizable and are carefully avoided. There is a fringe around the hunt meetings, however, who are the worst tramps in the world. Some rate the title "Gentlemen Riders" because they do not accept money for riding. These few unpleasant gentlemen will, on the other hand, usually accept money for anything else . . . money, entertainment, clothing or even remuneration for certain more dubious services. Since the owners at these racing-for-glory meetings are almost inevitably wealthy, a competent rider can do extremely well for himself by giving up the few dollars he might otherwise receive for his performance. "Mr. Parrish!" Well. Well.

The story went on.

> Parrish was badly hurt while riding at Laurel race track in Maryland in 1940, when he fell from a horse which had been entered in the name of his wife. Little is known of his activities from that time until he appeared in New York as Harry Lennen.

So Terry had had horses running in her name. They would have belonged either to Sam Eckman or to Lennen. Trainers usually list their horses under their wives' names because it entitles the ladies to an owner's badge so they can sit grandly among the elite while their husbands rassle with the critters below.

Then Eddie came in for a quote.

> Lieut. Marsh told reporters that he had confidently expected the crime to develop along lines which would involve the sporting element. Marsh said in part, "It has been apparent, from early in the Lennen investigation that some connection

would sooner or later appear between the murder
and the gambling fraternity. One of the first persons questioned after Lennen's body was found by
police was a character frequently seen in the company of Broadway undesirables and a well-known
figure at the local race tracks. The identification
of Lennen as a former jockey bears out our belief."

I debated suing Eddie for libel until I remembered that I
wasn't suing anybody for anything until I'd got myself out of
this jam.

The discovery that Terry was Lennen's wife seemed very
important, yet I didn't know what to do with it. Obviously Lennen hadn't changed his name because he didn't like it. It was
equally obvious that Terry wanted to . . . or had to . . . help
him in his deception.

One thing was certain. Whatever Harry Lennen had been
hiding from had finally caught up with him in the form of a
milk bottle. The sort of a guy Lennen had been . . . even since
his coming to New York . . . could have provided a hundred
reasons for people to wish him dead. Add to that the cheat-
ing and chiseling he'd probably done as Parrish, and you have
enough motives for a war. It wasn't impossible, either, that his
standing as Parrish would have led him into contacts in which
ten thousand dollar situations would be likely. I'd like to have
known the names of some of the people he'd ridden for down in
the hunting country. It could have been a rare spot for a touch
of blackmail.

There certainly weren't any Old Dominion gentlefolk on my
list of suspects . . . that parade of visitors to the corpse, my host
and young Fargo.

I went into the boy's room, took his temperature, let him
have some water and made up my mind that there were some
kinds of people you just couldn't kill. I sat down and wondered
what connection this boy could have had with Lennen . . . or
Parrish. Seven years ago he would have been . . . what? Fifteen?
Maybe sixteen, tops. He could have been around the tracks at

sixteen if he were under contract to someone with his parents' consent. That would make sense. Then, in around two years, he would have been drafted and disappear from the races. Seven years and a war is also quite a gap between a kid's getting sore at somebody and coming back to bop him over the head with a bottle. At the same time, the boy wasn't playing tag when somebody shot him. Fargo was in there all right, but I couldn't figure out where.

The telephone jangled downstairs. I waited a few seconds, said ho-hum or something, and went into the bathroom, closing the door behind me, and locking myself in. I was in no position to get caught eavesdropping at that stage of the game.

There was almost no noise below and I could hear clearly from the office. It was Pinky.

". . . you didn't lose much time using this number. I don't like it . . . who did? . . . when? . . . and he called you from Chicago? . . . all right, all right! Don't waste your time or mine telling me how tough it is! Find the guy that Kerschoff was tied up with. Somebody around here knows the deal . . . maybe a lot of people. There's a possibility this Parrish story may be a break as well as a threat. It's sure to start some talk in the trade about the deal. Make it a point to get around where you'll hear it . . . yes . . . I may. If I do, I'll call you as soon as I light anyplace. Bye."

I heard the sound of hanging up and of a door being opened. Pinky barked, "Mac!" It rang up our hall and my guard's feet clumped their way down. The office chair squeaked as Pinky sat down again. The laryngitic said, "Want me, boss?" Pinky said, "Close the door and wait a minute. I want you to go out and send a wire."

A drawer pulled out and slammed shut would be the telegraph blanks. A "goddammit" and the grinding of a pencil sharpener would be too much pressure . . . inside and out. It was a short message . . . maybe a minute until Pinky's chair squeaked back.

"Listen, Mac, and listen carefully." Pinky's voice was more intense than I'd ever heard it. "I'm going over this once . . . and that's all. The heat is on. The cops are combing the town for

me. They had no way, of connecting us with the Lennen thing
until they learned he was Parrish. Now we're hot . . . you understand? I'm wanted . . . by name, by description and by print. I
want you to send this wire from midtown . . . a small branch
office. Joe will drive you to the train and bring the car back.
When you get the wire off, I want you to get going . . . and keep
going. Understand?"

"But boss! I . . ."

"Will you shut up and do what you're told? You're not in this
business yet and I don't want you to get into it. Beat it before
I throw you out. Here's some dough . . ." Somebody turned the
juke-box on and, in a moment, I heard the office door close.
Feet followed on the stairs and I dropped down and unlocked
the bathroom, leaving Fargo's door closed for the moment. As I
walked into the room Pinky was standing on the threshold. I told
him to come in and turned to make a business of opening the
kid's door and straightening out his bed. When I got back, Pinky
had dropped into my big chair and was resting. Without opening
his eyes, he said, "What'd you think of the newspaper story?"

"I was pretty much surprised. Lennen had been something
of a mystery around the neighborhood for a couple of years."

"What about Terry Hale? You know her well?"

"No. I'd seen her around with Lennen. Then, as I told you,
she came to me when she thought the police were going to accuse her of the killing."

"But they didn't accuse her of the killing." Pinky opened his
eyes as he spoke. Closed them again.

"I think they're going to." I couldn't tell him now I knew. "I
think they'll hold her on whatever technicality they're holding
her on now until they charge her."

Pinky opened his eyes this time and kept them open. "You're
a little behind the times, Doc." I asked him what he meant.

"The police discharged Terry Hale tonight." He went into
the bathroom and got a drink of water while I thought that
over. "Yes. The cops let Terry Hale go tonight. From now on,
instead of being their number one suspect, she's to be their star
witness if my guess is any good."

I ambled over and poured myself a drink of Forester. I didn't need to ask Pinky against whom Terry would be a witness. His tone implied his concern. Then, "Well, happy days, Doc!" He made a gesture of tossing off an imaginary drink and I downed my Forester . . . saying nothing. After a while he seemed to relax a little. Maybe that's what made him so formidable. It wasn't an act. He could set his troubles aside when he needed to.

"I didn't wake you for your girl's program today. There weren't any personal messages this time."

"No? I thought the other one wasn't too well handled. I think she must have had it thrown at her the last minute. I've never heard Katie flustered before."

"Maybe she loves you."

"Always when I'm in a jam of some sort and never when I'm being respectable and serious."

"Ominous." Pinky laughed outright. It sounded like the old times of a couple of days ago. Where did a guy like that get words like ominous? "Well I'll get some sleep and be up to relieve you later."

"It won't be necessary. I can get by easily from now on so long as the kid keeps on doing so well."

"Okay, Doc. If I wake up I'll show. If not I'll sleep. Right?"

"Right. You look a little weary. Better sleep."

"By the way. The reason I brought up your girl's program is that you don't want to miss tomorrow's show. It's going to be extra special. She announced it today." Funny to see mischief sparkle in those hard eyes!

"Really? What's coming off?"

"Well, she's having a most unusual and fascinating guest artist. One she knows will *thrill* every listener with his *adventures* in living *dangerously.*"

"My God! Who?"

"Eddie Marsh."

18

Almost exactly at midnight as I was half drowsing beside Fargo, the telephone sounded off below. The boy had been sleeping lightly, off and on, and I made my dash for the ventilator a little less casual than usual. I locked the doors and climbed to my post. The big room was fairly quiet and Pinky's "Hello, Hello" had the semi-shouted quality we unconsciously use for long distance calls. Then there was a long pause. Finally Pinky spoke.

"Okay. You couldn't have done anything else. I don't blame you. They knew all the answers before they asked you the questions. Forget it and get yourself in the clear. You won't want any part of me from here in. . . . You might as . . ." More protest, apparently, from the other end. "You might as well forget it, I tell you, because, if you don't you'll be in a mess that will close you up . . . and worse. This whole thing is going to break today and I haven't got a prayer." Pinky's voice didn't express the resigned quality of the things he said. There was a terrible, quiet purpose in every word he spoke . . . spacing out those words with a bitter finality that meant his listener was to understand once and for all. "Don't try to get in touch with me any more. I won't be here. Don't try to help, no matter what happens. You don't know why, but your testimony would come damned close to hanging me . . . and just remember what I've told you before. There aren't enough cops in the state to take me back. I won't *go* back. I've had enough. Thanks, kid. So long."

That was it. Putting the two conversations together, the one with a local person . . . probably the lawyer . . . and the other with someone out of town he'd wired to call him, it didn't take much reasoning to figure that Eddie Marsh had tied Pinky up directly with Lennen's death.

I'm not too imaginative and I think I've got about as much nerve as the next guy, but I found my hands cold slippery-wet on the shower rail and my whole being looking for some way to get out of there. At least I'm realist enough to know that a guy who's that close to being convicted of murder isn't going to worry about the safety of any of the people who might be able to hang him. I'm realist enough to know that when a guy like Pinky says there aren't enough cops in the state to take him back, it isn't going to be healthy for the people who happen to be around him when the cops try it. And, of course, try it they would. According to Pinky, within the next day or so.

I was thinking what Katie's broadcast might develop; and about the fact that we'd be moving somewhere else; and about Fargo's condition, when I heard Pinky climbing the stairs. I busied myself around and tried to be as natural as I could. He came in quietly, closed and locked the door without speaking. I'd retreated to Fargo's room and said, "That you?" He said, "Yes," and I heard the big chair squeak, then the striking of a match. I called, "Be in in a minute." He didn't answer.

When I'd stalled off some of my nervousness . . . at least some of the tension that showed . . . I strolled back. Nothing was said for a time and I sat down. I remarked, "The boy's better."

"That's good. He'll need to be better. We're moving." Pinky dragged at his cigarette and ground it out. I said, "When?" He got up and walked around. "I'm not sure. Soon."

"You can't leave the boy behind?"

"I can't leave anybody behind." He glanced suddenly at me as though I'd proposed his turning me loose. "That's the hell of it. I can't leave anybody behind." He turned his back again and absently snapped the radio switch on and off without playing anything. "You know, of course, that I'm taking this thing away from you."

"I can't stop you . . . if that's the way you want it." For the first time since I'd known Pinky, I got a feeling that I'd like to slug him . . . to take him . . . to slap him into the can with a murder charge against him. All the phony amenities with which he had put me off my guard irked the hell out of me. The guy may have fancied himself as smooth or something, but I wasn't having any more of it. He said, "Well, that's the way I want it."

There wasn't any answer to that one so I burned silently. A party had come in downstairs and the place got noisy all at once. The lousy band played its lousy tunes and the lousy slot machines collected their lousy quarters. The milk of human kindness soured in its crock.

I needn't kid myself any longer about the whole nasty business. From here in every play was for keeps and the guy who finally picked up the marbles would know he'd been through something. I had no doubt that Eddie Marsh would be the man to walk off with the marbles, all right, but I was quite a lot concerned with the wreckage he might leave behind. Pinky's voice startled me.

"You understand, of course, that Eddie Marsh will be sending you a direct message from Katie Storm's broadcast tomorrow."

"I suppose so."

"It is to my advantage that I hear it and you don't." He pulled the plug out of the baseboard and wrapped the cord, with the antenna wire, around the set. "I'll be right back and relieve you."

"I don't need relief tonight." I was still burning, didn't think I'd be able to sleep and certainly didn't want to sit up with this guy all night.

"You may not need relief, Doc, but you can use a little watching." I didn't like Pinky's grin any more. If I'd ever thought it was infectious, I was nuts. It was poison. "I'm a man short at the moment and I'd prefer to know that you'd have to get the key out of my pocket before you could leave."

He walked out, carefully locking the door after him.

I listened to his steps down to the first floor with a growing and violent rage. For the first time, I felt my bonds really chafing.

Okay. If I had to spend the night with the guy, I'd do it my way. See as little of him as possible. I checked on Fargo and took a shower. By the time Pinky had come back I was ready for bed. He locked the door from the inside this time.

We said nothing. There was nothing to say. Pinky simply went into Fargo's room and settled down to his thoughts and plans. I turned out my light and lay down to some thoughts and plans of my own. The thinking and planning went on until the cars started driving away from the club.

When the dishwasher started his lonely choruses of *Shantytown*, the thoughts and plans had resolved themselves into one thought and no plan.

I was going to get the hell out of there!

I was still there in the morning when I woke to find my breakfast and no Pinky. Fargo said he had brought it a few minutes before and left, making somewhat of a clatter which, I suppose, was intended to wake me.

I was still there when the endless morning had ended and the endless hour had begun until Katie's show was due. I had heard no signs of radio at any time in the house and wondered, without hoping too hard for fear of disappointment, if the set could possibly be in the office.

I was still there when, at one o'clock, I stood on the rim of the bath tub and heard that sweet, familiar voice come clearly up to me from the big set in the office. The opening announcement by the guy I dislike boomed up like a public address system . . . then the office chair squeaked and the volume came down. Another squeak and I knew I had Pinky located for the next half hour. Katie stuck to her regular formula . . . telling about her guest early in the program and interviewing him later.

> My guest today brings you an intimate picture of
> a world far removed from the lives of most of us
> . . . a world in which the forces of law meet and
> defeat the forces of crime. As he sits in the studio,
> Lieutenant Edward Marsh of the Police Depart-

ment of the City of New York, looks very much
like a successful . . . and, may I add, very distinguished . . . business man. Actually, this quiet
citizen is the same gallant Eddie Marsh who ran
down and shot it out with the notorious Gillard
brothers only four years ago. Ladies, may I introduce Police Lieutenant Detective Edward Marsh!

And for this, the gallant Eddie peeps, "How do you do." I'd
forgotten his shooting affray with the Gillards. Funny thing
about people like Eddie. You forget they're ever mixed up in
stuff like that. Maybe he was getting ready for some more shooting. Well, Pinky isn't the sort of guy to hold you in *front* of him
while they were shooting it out, but he'd damn well see that you
weren't *behind* him. It was pretty disturbing.

Katie worked through her "Presto Insole" plug and made
a neat transition to Eddie. "I don't know whether our guest
has ever tried shoes with our 'Presto Insole,' but I'm sure they
would be a great comfort to the men of the finest police department in the world."

The dumb announcer said, "Surely, Katie, you don't refer to
the old saw that 'all policemen have big feet!'"

Eddie, who has approximately the biggest feet I ever saw on
a man his size, said, "Most of us have, Miss Storm. If you don't
have big feet when you start out as a cop, you soon get 'em!"
Whereupon everybody went "Ha, ha, ha!" So they got him off to
some sort of a start by bringing up the business man thing and
Eddie said most of a detective's work was like a business man's
and very little of it shooting. He also expressed a conservative
preference for more time at his desk and less time shooting it
out with people. It was all very nice until Katie cued him into
the subject at hand with, "Aren't you working on something
quite dramatic right now, Lieutenant Marsh? The Lennen murder case, isn't it?"

"Yes. The Lennen case has taken on some rather dramatic
aspects in the last twenty-four hours. In fact I am indebted to
you and your sponsors for this time on the air, not as a personal

gratification, but as a real and valued service to the Police Department."

Katie said, "How exciting!"

No question about it. They were reading a prepared script. Not only that, but it had been rehearsed. Nobody could have droned through it in the monotonous way Eddie did, without having read it over to the point of exhaustion. Just one word after another.

"Yes, Miss Storm, Harry Lennen, whom we now know as Frank Parrish, a former jockey, was found dead in his apartment, last Monday night, after the police had received a mysterious telephone call. The person who made that call had, only a few moments before, seen Lennen's body and had, undoubtedly, examined it. He was a man who would have understood what he saw. We have no way of knowing how much this person may have learned during his visit, nor whom he may have encountered while in or near Lennen's apartment."

Katie said, "It sounds terribly mysterious!"

"Some of the mystery, however, is cleared up, Miss Storm. The identity of the person who made the call . . . and visited Lennen's apartment . . . is positively known to the police."

Damn! Eddie didn't sound as though it was a gag, either. He went on reading with the sort of oxlike determination to get it over with, that people get in front of microphones.

"The Police Department has reason to believe that this person has come into the possession of facts which constitute a grave threat to his life so long as the murderer of Harry Lennen remains at large."

"How dreadful! Isn't there some way to warn the person?"

"We hope there is. We know that, if a radio is available to him, he will be listening to your broadcast."

"I'm flattered!"

"You may well be, Miss Storm. He is a great admirer of yours. Yes, it is our hope that he will be hearing us today . . . whether he is in hiding or whether, as we have reason to fear, he may be in the hands of the killer. He has completely disappeared and has, so far, failed to communicate with the authorities."

"You speak of the killer, Lieutenant Marsh. Do the police know who the killer is?"

"Definitely. It will remain for the courts to decide his guilt or innocence, but there is no question, in my opinion, of the identity of the murderer. The testimony of witnesses places him in the company of the murdered man thirty minutes before the crime and also places him at Lennen's apartment at the very moment of the killing."

"Don't police look for a motive in establishing the identity of a murderer . . . I mean, have you discovered a reason for the crime."

"We have discovered a very close connection between Harry Lennen's past life as Frank Parrish and that of the man we intend to arrest. Yes. I think I may say that the motive, in this case, is very clear."

"Lieutenant Marsh. Isn't it somewhat unusual for the Police Department to make statements of this sort over the air? It's tremendously interesting but is it . . . official?"

"I'm glad you asked me that question, Miss Storm, because it is not only unusual but is actually unprecedented. But it is definitely official. Obviously all this information will be released to the press, but we are hoping it may reach the man whom we fear is being held by the murderer."

"And you say that, during the period of this man's absence, you have had no contact with him, directly or undirectly?" Katie threw it at him. Obviously this wasn't in the script because Eddie fell all over himself. You could see him looking up and losing his place.

"Why . . . no. No. . . . None whatever."

"And you have had no hint whatever as to where he may be or what he may be doing?"

"None. We would have followed it up immediately."

Good old Katie! At least Pinky would be smart enough to know that Katie had thrown that in to let me know she'd kept the faith. Bless her heart! She went back to the script. . . . I could picture her stalling long enough for Marsh to try to find his line.

"And so, Lieutenant Marsh, this fascinating guest appearance you've made here today is actually in the nature of a warning to a man who may be in extreme danger?"

Eddie never found his place. After a moment of hesitation, he plunged into an ad lib . . . probably his first, undoubtedly, his last. He really sweat it out. "Yes. A warning . . . of the most . . . serious nature. I want him to know that the brutal killer of Harry Lennen is also the convicted killer of another man. He killed another man for the same reason he killed Lennen. That man he beat to death. I can't emphasize it strongly enough . . . that warning . . . Doc . . . this fella'll *kill* you! If you're free, *stay out of his way!* Get in touch with me at once. If you're not . . . GET AWAY FROM HIM!"

Then, they tell me, there was something else. In the confusion of small sounds from the studio audience at Marsh's unintentional dramatic climax, I thought I'd misheard. To me, up my ventilator shaft, it sounded for all the world as though Katie had sobbed, "Jimmy! . . . Oh, Jimmy!"

She had. From Coast to Coast.

From then on it was pretty much of a clambake. The announcer jumped in and put up a yap about being happy to be of service to the Police Department, thanked everybody for everybody else, listed the sponsors and gave Katie time to collect herself and get off the air about as usual.

I heard the office radio switch snapped off and the office chair squeak. A door closing made a soft thud. Almost at once a heavy, deliberate tread began to mount toward me. I stood in the middle of my room and waited until I heard the key in the door. Then the man stood there on the threshold . . . his face a calm, worn mask . . . his eyes steadily on mine.

Then I realized that I was facing a man convicted of beating one person to death, who had probably slaughtered Harry Lennen with a milk bottle, and whose quiet expression could hide all these things until the instant of their execution.

I realized, then, that I was facing a killer.

19

After Katie's broadcast Pinky had said nothing. He was with Fargo as I sat down in my room and contemplated the possibility . . . or the seeming impossibility . . . of escape. Boards on the windows. Old fashioned but thoroughly effective locks on the two doors. Four possible avenues of egress. I couldn't go out through the walls or the ventilator. I simply had to choose one of the four impossibles and, somehow, make it possible.

Once free . . . anyplace . . . anyplace I could get to a phone, I could have the house quietly taken over by the police. If Pinky got away, the sick Fargo could at least be taken to a hospital where he belonged. It wasn't for me to concern myself with the cops' business any longer. Sooner or later, Eddie would arrest the right person and the courts would convict him. All I had to do was get out of there.

It was one forty-five. Pinky's preparations for getting away couldn't very well start until the place closed at three tomorrow morning . . . or, as sometimes happened, earlier. Thirteen hours. The business-as-usual policy had been, of course, to avoid attracting any sudden attention to the club. With the man-hunt on in earnest, they'd not vary their rule tonight. Friday night might be busy. It generally is in that sort of joint. A busy night there is a noisy one . . . and I'd need a noisy one for my purposes.

I'd need a noisy night, especially if I chose the window in my room. Both the window and the door of Fargo's room were out of consideration under any plan I could bring myself to make. I wouldn't have hesitated to inject Pinky with anything in the book while I tore the house down. But the kid was my patient . . .

The bathroom door opened and I heard Pinky say, "Okay, kid, keep your chin up. See you later." He came on through without a glance in my direction. As he opened the door, he apparently thought better of it and faced me seriously. "Your friend, Marsh, made a great point on the radio program of the necessity for your escape."

I said, "Yes?"

Pinky said, "Yes." Then, very distinctly, he said, "Don't try it." He took the key from his pocket, unlocked the door and was gone. I heard the lock rattle on the outside and followed his footfalls into the quiet house below.

Something, just then, tried to attract my attention. Something about something that had just happened. A flash . . . the little bell ringing . . . the fleeting feeling that I should realize something that I hadn't realized. I found out what it was later.

As I worked around Fargo, he said, "Well, Doc, I hear we're moving out." I told him yes and that I didn't like it at all. He thought this over. "You don't like it on account of it might be bad for me?"

"I don't like it on account of it will be bad for both of us. It certainly won't do you any good and I'm getting to be a worse headache to all of you all the time."

"You ain't any headache to me, Doc. I don't count you in at all." The boy's face looked as though he were burdened with some overwhelming responsibility. It was funny in a gentle sort of way. "You did my operation and I'm getting all right. I know I'm getting all right, now. That's all you were supposed to do. That was what it was at first. Now it's different. Now the boss says you'll go to the cops just as soon as you get out, so he can't let you out. That ain't your fault. You're the kind of a guy you are and the boss can't change that."

"That's right, Fargo. He knows I'd go to the police. From his point of view he's right." I wondered if this kid was cooking up some way of helping me. I couldn't let him. He'd have to lie

there in his bed and take the consequences. With the Pinky I
was learning to know, the consequences wouldn't be pretty. Fargo continued to look puzzled. I felt that he was coming around
to some sort of a statement, so I started collecting loose stuff
that would need to be packed. I had no intention of taking anything with me, but I wanted to look ready if Pinky came back
that afternoon. Then I heard the voice from the bed. "Doc."

I said, yes, and wandered around where I could look at him.
"Come over here . . . kind of close." His voice was low and he
glanced at the door. I sat at the bedside and leaned over him.

"Doc." He scratched his head again. "I'm no rat, see." He
obviously was struggling with unfamiliar words and ideas.
"There ain't anything in the world that would make me . . . I
don't exactly know how to put it . . ."

"That would make you betray a trust, Fargo?"

"Yeah. Yeah. That would make me betray a trust, like." Relieved, he went on. "But I still figure that some things are right
and some ain't. I mean things that are right for us . . . Pinky
and me . . . might not be right for you. See?"

"I think so, kid. But look here. I don't want you getting into
any trouble. You're in no shape to . . . to take care of yourself
if you get in a jam."

"It ain't a case of getting into a jam. What I been trying to
figure out is all in my own head. It would only be between you
and me."

Well, there it was. What he'd been trying to figure out in
his own head was a stiff problem in his sort of ethics . . . pretty
rigorous exercise for that head. I've seen a lot of guys well up
in the scale of the behavers who took their ethics less seriously
than this youngster with an illegal bullet-hole in his belly. I
suggested that maybe he'd better tell me about it.

"Tell me, Doc. If you could get out of here before we are
supposed to leave tonight, would you promise me to hide someplace 'til we was gone . . . 'til morning, say?" He didn't look up.
"Hide someplace and not call the cops?"

There it is for you, Doc! Right on the line. The kid knows
some way for you to get out. You can promise the boy and get

away. Then you can call the cops. That, of course, is your civic duty. You can be comforted by the smug thought that it's for everybody's best good. Or you can promise the boy and be a sentimental ass by keeping your promise and trying to explain it to Eddie Marsh who is not sympathetic to that sort of thing. Or you can be noble . . . and probably dead. Who's giving the ethics lesson to whom? I heard myself saying, "No, I'm afraid I wouldn't, Fargo. I'd probably break my promise and call the cops. I'll work it out some other way."

He didn't seem put out. His puzzled expression was gone and he looked as if something had amused him . . . just a sly twinkle. He looked a little like a wise old man. I couldn't make him out for a moment. Then he said:

"You know it's funny. I knew you would say that. It would have been all right if you'd said yes, but it's better this way." I asked him why it was better that way.

"Because it leaves it up to me. If you find a way to get out of here tonight I can give you as much time as I want . . . or as little. I'm supposed to watch you. Pinky gave me a penny to put in the light socket here in the bed lamp if anything goes wrong. That blows the fuse. Pinky's got to go over to the place we're moving to and make sure it's okay. From the time his car goes out the back I'm to watch you and listen; See?"

"I see." I wondered what he had in his mind. "But what's to prevent me from tying you up or doping you or something to take advantage of what you've just told me?"

"The same thing that stopped you from making a deal with me not to call the cops." He grinned happily at his wisdom. "You'll try to get away somehow. I don't know how . . . but somehow. There won't be much guard around for an hour or so. You'll go. Then, before you have time to get the cops out here, I'll blow the fuse. You won't take the penny away from me because you think Pinky will slap hell out of me if it's gone. See?"

I saw.

While we were grinning at each other, we heard Pinky coming up again and I beat it for the other room. He walked straight in and stood with his back to the open door. He was all business.

"You can take all your stuff your instruments and such. What you leave behind will be thrown away. These rooms will have been taken to pieces and old furniture stored in them before morning. We are leaving at three-forty-five or four at the latest."

I said I was partly packed and he made a quick inspection trip with his eyes. Then he said, "Don't get funny and try anything," and he was gone.

Once again, as he locked the door, I got that feeling that I should be paying attention to something. This time it didn't get away from me. I waited until Pinky's steps had disappeared. Then I waited until I was sure no one else was climbing the stairs. The thing that had attracted my attention was the fact that I hadn't heard the small scratch of the key as it was removed from the door and the instant's hesitation of the steps outside while it was being dropped into a pocket. I tiptoed to the door and peeked through the keyhole. There, as I'd suddenly hoped, was the butt of the key. There was the key, ready to be turned from my side with whatever would reach in there and turn it. Or ready to be pushed through and caught, as it dropped, by a newspaper slid, under the door . . . then to be pulled inside for the unlocking job.

Well, well! The Mastermind's slip was showing! He'd probably got so used to having that hall full of henchmen that he'd become careless. Maybe he didn't credit me with enough savvy to remember the oldest gag in the housebreaker's handbook. On the other hand, there was probably a large party named Joe waiting at the foot of the stairs with a blackjack or worse. Time enough to worry about that later. All I had to do was find something to work that key with and then I could go to work on the problem of Joe and his blackjack. I might arrange a blackjack of my own.

For a guy with a good pair of thin, tool-steel tweezers in his bag, I wasted an extraordinary lot of time trying to think of some way to get hold of the key-butt. Then I dug into my gear and found it. A preliminary test showed me that I could turn the key easily . . . not enough actually to unlock the door, but plenty to line it up so that it would push through. So far, so good.

There were things to be taken along. Not many, but damned important things. There was a pencil-beam flashlight from my bag. I had a spare battery to take in my pocket. I had plenty of change, including nickels, for the phone. A four-ounce bottle, rinsed out, insured a couple of drinks of Forester for the road. Came, then, the problem of a weapon. I made the rounds of both rooms on one pretext or another in search of something which would do. It must be small, silent and effective.

While I was thinking of taking the table lamp to pieces and using the base, the casters on the bureau caught my eye. Four of them, quite heavy. They wouldn't be missed in a casual inspection. I gave a listen below and pulled them out without much difficulty. Together, they made a very respectable and solid total. I hid the flashlight and bottle under my pillow and went to work on my weapon.

There was a huge lot of adhesive tape and plenty of bandage. As logical and useful camouflage, I changed Fargo's dressing and made him an emergency traveling corset which would give him a reasonable amount of protection. When I retired to my room again, I left I some of the adhesive and bandage strewn around.

I bound the casters together tightly with the tape, making a compact ball of them. Then I wrapped them a number of times in gauze bandage, leaving eight or nine inches of gauze trailing out for a handle. When I had sufficient bandage folded back and forth to make a fairly thick core for the handle, I started wrapping the whole arrangement with layer after layer of adhesive tape. When I'd finished, the thing looked like some stone-age bludgeon and felt equally effective. It was a little bulky, but I found I could hide it pretty well under my belt, sucking my belly a little and buttoning my coat. You've carried a quart that way, maybe.

I added my weapon to the little collection under my pillow and sat down to wait out the long evening. Fargo had said little while I'd done his dressing . . . and nothing at all about our talk of the afternoon. A tray was set in front of the door about eight and I was invited to pick it up when the door was opened. Then the door was closed, locked and the man was gone. Probably Joe. I held my breath literally, until I peeked through and saw the key still there. Anyway, Joe wasn't too shrewd.

I ate little and probably shouldn't have eaten that. The club downstairs filled up. If I wanted a noisy evening, I got it. Everything was going at once and we had an epidemic of steaks and smoke. I didn't hear any footsteps on the stairs and figured the guarding was being done from down there. I wondered if it would be that way after Pinky went out on his errand.

It was.

It was exactly two o'clock that morning . . . that next morning . . . when I heard the car start up and leave the back of the house. I listened a while for footsteps that didn't come. Then I slid yesterday's newspaper under the door, eased the key out of the lock, heard it hit the floor and prayed silently that it had stayed on the paper. When I pulled it back, there it was.

Before I unlocked the door, I made a final check of Fargo's room and the other door. Everything seemed okay. As I started to close the bathroom door again, he looked up and said, "So long, Doc, and thanks."

I laughed, I guess. It seemed so damned silly. It seemed, also, kind of decent and solid and unlike everything which had surrounded me in the last few days. "So long, Fargo. Thank you, too. I'll be seeing you when this is straightened out. Don't let 'em bounce you around too much . . . and whatever you do, stay down flat."

"Okay, Doc." Then, as an afterthought, "I didn't kill nobody, Doc. You'll know that sometime."

"I know it now, kid. Hang on to that penny and remember, we haven't got any deals . . . either way."

"No deals, Doc." I closed the bathroom door on my patient and gathered up my stuff. Then my carefully planned routine . . . light out in the bathroom; light out in the bedroom; a look through the keyhole as soon as my eyes had accommodated themselves to the darkness. The hall showed almost no light. I waited until I was certain my eyes were right and looked again. The only light seemed to be coming from below. There could, possibly, be a dim globe somewhere in the far end of the narrow space.

I unlocked the door quietly, although the dance band and the crowd downstairs would have covered a lot more sound. There might be someone on guard in the hall, but, unless he had come up extremely carefully, I doubted it. The steps were noisy. I'd have to watch that. The steps were noisy and bare.

In the darkness I knew that nothing would show when I opened the door except the moving door itself. If anybody was watching that door from the hall, I'd find out quick. I opened it a crack with my left hand and stepped back with my sap in the right. Nothing happened. With my toe I pushed it a little farther. The hall seemed light after the room, but it was, I knew, quite dark to anyone from the lighted area below.

I slid out and carefully closed the door. I looked back of me and saw no one. But I did see a window. There was a shade over it. I also saw something else. As I turned away from the window to check the stairs, I saw Joe. He was leaning back in a chair . . . leaning back against the wall in the full light at the foot of the stairway. He was reading a magazine. He didn't look too big or too tough, but he definitely looked too far down those stairs for any surprise attack. I went back to inspect the window. As I pulled the shade back an inch, I saw my answer at once. No good. Bars. Solid bars in a steel frame. The place had probably been used for gambling at some time.

That left only the stairs. There wasn't any time to waste and I became increasingly afraid Fargo would think I was away and blow the fuse. I wondered how many circuits in the house . . . what lights were on the circuit which lighted the upstairs. There had to be enough lights below which would go out to give the warning. Pinky wouldn't have missed that.

I made up my mind. The situation couldn't be a whole lot worse than it was and I'd have to take a big chance no matter how I went about it. I had to get Joe off his can and moving before I would have a prayer. If he left his post for a minute I

wouldn't know where he was. If he came up here, I could sap
him and run for it.

I went back into my room and locked the door. I closed both
bathroom doors behind me as I went into Fargo's room. He
looked surprised but didn't say anything. I told him, "I'm going
out this way, Fargo. It'll be better all around. When I give you
the word, I want you to blow the fuses. I'll wait until Joe comes
into my room, then go out from here. That way, you can tell
him exactly what happened. That way you'll be in the clear."
The kid puzzled a moment.

"Ain't that a little close, Doc?"

"Not as close as it looks out there now. It's the best way.
Will you do it?"

"All I do is blow the fuse when you tell me?"

"That's all."

"Sure, Doc. Anything you say." He came up with his penny
and a nervous grin. I told him to hold it, turned out his light,
and slipped back to my room, unlocked the door and eased into
the hall. I locked the door behind me and slid down the wall in
the shadow. I had left the key in its accustomed position in the
door. When I came to Fargo's door, I carefully unlocked it and
slipped into the darkened room. He whispered, "Doc?" I said,
"Yeah. Wait." I closed the door and locked it from the inside.

The bed lamp was off and I used my pencil flashlight to
insert Fargo's penny into the socket and screw in the lamp. It
needed only switching on in order to short-circuit the line. I
said, "Are you set, kid?" He whispered, "Any time, Doc." I waited
for a loud chorus from the band below and said, "Let 'em go,
Fargo!"

There was a sound in the lamp, followed by a loud rum-
pus below. I held my hand on the key and tried to control my
breathing while I heard a shout through the hall and a pair of
feet pounded up the stairs . . . one pair. The feet banged past
Fargo's door as I'd hoped. I heard hurried fumbling at the lock
of my door, then heard it open. I went out into the hall . . .
shot my flash at the other door, standing open . . . closed and
locked Fargo's door from the outside and dashed up the hall to

my door just as I heard Joe fumbling through the bathroom. Fargo was yelling, "Joe! In here, Joe!" I locked my door after a lot of groping in the dark and headed for the stairs. I had both keys in my pocket.

There was a lot of running around down there but the band was still playing loud and bad in the big room. A little light was coming up the stairway from someplace and I got down clumsily. I ran into some guy . . . a waiter I guess . . . who was trying to strike a match. He said, "What the hell!" I said, "Some kina trouble' up there. Better go see."

I ran toward the back of the house. As I passed one door I could see the blue and orange spitting of a steak broiling over charcoal. I ducked in and said, "Where the hell's the fuse box?" Somebody said, "On the porch." Somebody else said, "Pete's fixing it. What's all the fuss?" By that time I was through the screen door and on the porch. The man with the flashlight must be Pete. Without turning away from the fuse box he said, "That you, Dutch?" I said, "Yeah."

I hit the dirt from the steps and headed away from the house.

The sounds back of me faded as I stumbled toward freedom.

20

I guess I'm a city guy.

Between the roadhouse and what seemed to be a patch of woods about a quarter of a mile away, I fell over everything but a corpse. I even did the barrel-hoop gag and banged my right shin a wallop that made me forget the rest of my troubles for a minute. A barbed-wire fence, despite a lot of expensive army training I'd been given to avoid it, bit me at random. As I turned back to pull my pants off the thing, I saw that the lights had gone back on in the kitchen. Not a glimmer from the boarded upper windows to tell me whether Joe had been rescued yet.

The woods looked pretty much like going no place and I skirted around the edge. There must have been some wet low-land not far away because I could hear frogs. I headed away from that, knowing it wouldn't be too good a gamble for a house and a telephone.

There was no moon and I could see only an occasional star but there seemed to be light enough for me to distinguish the larger masses. Larger, that is, than barrel hoops and fences. No street lights anyplace. No house that I could make out except the one I didn't want any further part of. I kept going until I'd put the woods between me and the place.

My watch dial glowed two-twenty. Pinky had been away twenty minutes. At least he could hardly be on my trail for a while. I wondered how many people at the roadhouse had any knowledge of what was going on . . . people working there.

My guess was that they would run their club and, as Pinky had suggested, mind their own business. That left a one-man posse, for half an hour or so, on my heels. There was a hell of a lot of acreage out there and a hell of a lot of directions for Joe to take unless he had a bloodhound. Joe didn't worry me too much. What worried me was the problem of where I was and where I was going.

Somewhere I heard the sound of a car . . . up ahead of me. A flip of light showed between the trees and then I saw headlights as they described a road running at right angles to my course, maybe another quarter of a mile off. I headed toward the road. It had to lead someplace where there would be a house. I could follow a telephone line and stop at the first place where I found wires coming off it to a building.

I floundered endlessly through weeds up to here. Plenty of them must have been nettle or thistle or something. They took over where the barbed-wire had left off. The car had long since gone and I plugged on with only a memory of the location of the highway. A steep upgrade led me to a fence. I crawled over it and found a third-class macadam road.

It didn't take long to discover that there weren't any telephone poles. I wasn't too annoyed because at least I was free. I felt better and better about the whole thing as I swung down the road keeping an eye out for lights . . . ready to duck at the first suspicious sound . . . ready to sap somebody with my warclub if necessary. It felt heavy and comforting in my coat pocket.

For a while, anyway, direction didn't count much as long as it was away from where I was. I shagged along at a fair pace for what I guessed to be about fifteen minutes and came to another road . . . not much better, but with poles of some sort. A truck, roaring by, found me hiding in the ditch along the road, wishing I'd hailed it.

A little farther on, a good concrete highway appeared and at the corner was a sign which read, "New York, 43 Mi." Forty-three miles! Mister, do you know how much open country you can get yourself into within forty-three miles of New York?

Plenty. Take my word for it. What's more, this was it and it looked like it would be a fair kind of a jaunt to get to a phone . . . if I knew where there was a phone.

I heard a motor up the road, a car headed for the city and I grabbed the little flashlight out of my pocket and stood by. When the headlights came in sight I waggled the thing at them from the middle of the road. No soap. I jumped out of the way and he roared by me like a fast freight. It was just that . . . another truck. It was probably loaded with nice fresh eggs for the civilized breakfasts of civilized people who lived on Katie's side of town and kept out of murders.

I'd walked another half mile without seeing any signs of anything useful when I heard another car coming slower. I repeated my mid-road wig-wagging and this one slowed down and stopped. The guy in the car looked me over suspiciously. I said, "How about a ride?" He said, "Where are you going?" I told him I was trying to find a telephone and that I'd appreciate it if he'd take me down the road to someplace where I could find one. He put a flashlight full in my face. After being startled I tried to look honest. I must have succeeded because he opened the door and invited me in.

"A telephone? Sure! I'm on my way to where there's a phone right now. I don't like to pick up people at night but you look honest."

I said thanks and he pulled out and headed down the road, while I reached for a cigarette. Man, what a relief! The guy snapped in the lighter and said, "It comes out when it's hot." I offered him a smoke and he took one. When he put the glowing lighter up to his face I could make out his features for the first time because he'd been driving without his dashlight. An ordinary looking guy. He talked a little tough but seemed glad of the company. I should be choosy at that hour in the morning!

"You broke down?"

"Not exactly. I got separated from my party in a sort of a drunken mix-up and I want to find out where they went." I must have seemed too sober to the guy because he wanted to know more about it.

"You don't look drunk enough for that kind of a shindig."

"I don't drink much. Not as much as my friends." I bethought me of my four ounces of Forester. "I could buy you a little drink right now if you'd like." I hauled out the bottle and waited.

"No thanks. Go ahead, though, help yourself." I did, and half of my four ounces of liquor warmly celebrated my escape. One telephone call to Headquarters and one to Katie. Then one to a cab outfit. Then home and breakfast.

I heard the voice beside me. "We turn off here." We turned off there. It was another third-class road with no poles. I said, "They've got a telephone there, have they?"

"Oh sure. They've got a telephone and they'll probably have a cup of coffee for us. It's my brother's place. He's got a farm down here a ways." In a little while he turned left again on a road where there was a telephone line and I felt better. In a few hundred yards he slowed down and I could make out a mailbox and a farm gate ahead. He swung his wheel and cut into the place up a bumpy lane. In some trees above us I could see the bulk of a white house. When the headlights hit it, I could tell that it was quite small and pretty well run down. The yard was overgrown and the place littered with junk. The guy's brother wasn't much of a farmer. But there was a telephone lead-in at the side of the house.

We pulled up and got out. The guy said, "This way," and took my arm. "Look out for the stuff lying around. My brother just moved in and hasn't had time to clean up yet."

The house was dark as we climbed the front steps and knocked. There was no bell on the door but there was one in my head. I had a notion to break and run for it. Then I heard somebody inside come to the door and a muffled "Who is it?" The guy with me said, "It's me. I brought a fella who wants to use the phone." The man inside said, "Wait a minute," and I heard the door being unlocked. Then we went in.

Funny. There was a light inside . . . yet not any had shown from the porch. Not so funny, there was a guy standing in front of us in the half shadow with a gun in his hand.

It was Pinky.

I was too startled to speak. Did I say startled? I have been startled by a cough in a library reading room. I was stiff with all the fright a guy can handle before he gets limp. Tableau! The film had stopped and the picture just sat there. I couldn't talk and the other guy . . . it had to be Joe . . . was probably as scared as I when he got a look at Pinky's face.

Pinky said, "How'd you get here, Doc?" Nobody could have said, "I'll blow your brains out," any nastier. Joe started to break out with, "It was this way, boss . . ." and Pinky said, "Shut up! How'd you get here, Doc?"

I got my legs under me and managed to make some sort of vocal sounds. "I broke out and got away. I'd got 'way off from the place. Then I thumbed a ride with this guy." Pinky didn't even grin . . . not even that nasty number he puts on once in a while. He snapped like a dog at Joe . . . like a big dog.

"How long was he loose?"

"Loose? Why . . ." Stupid and frightened.

Pinky said, "Goddammit, let's have it! How long was he away from the club before you picked him up?" Then Joe chattered like a gibbon.

"Maybe half an hour. Not more. He didn't get to a phone because he was looking for one when I found him." It was as much of a plea for mercy as a statement. Big, dumb laryngitic Mac would have been worth a dozen of this fellow. "That's the first thing he asked me."

The man with the gun walked out of the shadow and stood directly in front of me. "Go in the other room." I walked ahead of him into a dirty place with a couch and a couple of chairs sitting untidily around. There was a kitchen table in the middle and some newspapers spread out on it. Pinky motioned to a chair. "Sit down." I sat down. "Go over him, Joe." Joe went over me, depositing my treasures on the table, one by one. Pinky picked up the sap and weighed it in his hand. I never realized how vicious it could look. He did laugh, then, and started peeling the tape off the handle. Joe pulled out my remaining drink of Forester and said, "He offered me some of this. I was afraid it was doped."

Pinky got something out of his pocket and threw it on the table. The guy must have been born with a gun in his fist. He wasn't even awkward as he worked with the other hand. That damned hole down the barrel kept looking me straight between the eyes. The thing he threw on the table was a roll of picture wire. "I brought a few things along, too. Wire him to the chair, Joe. Hands back of him through the spokes, feet through the rungs." I went cold . . . colder . . . inside.

Joe got to work. He hurt like hell and I squawked. Pinky told him, "You don't have to cut a guy to pieces when you tie him that way. Just make it solid and hurry it up." He made it solid. When he stood up, I couldn't move without tearing my wrists and ankles wide open. Pinky taped my mouth shut with adhesive from my weapon, then walked up and pushed me over with his foot. I lit on my side on the floor with the wires biting into my flesh. I knew I'd stay there until somebody cut me loose. I couldn't see Pinky but I could hear him.

"All right, let's go. I'll need you with me. Drive your car around to the machine shed in back so it can't be seen from the lane. The station wagon's back there. Drive it out."

I heard them walk away and listened to Pinky moving around the house while Joe carried out his orders. After a time there was a car outside and Joe came in the front way. Nothing was said as they went out and drove away.

I shall not record my thoughts and such utterances as I could mumble inside my tape. There was a great many of them and they weren't very original. They went on for something like forty-five minutes, and were largely concerned with whether I was to be left to rot in an abandoned farmhouse or whether they were coming back to shoot me. Before the three quarters of an hour were up, I was praying for them to come back and make me take care of Fargo again.

I had no more illusions about Pinky's place in the picture or about the methods he'd use to avoid arrest. I felt certain that Fargo had told me the truth when he'd said that he'd "never killed nobody." Pinky had to know that. It made a cheap liar of him . . . the kind who would pose and sentimentalize to make himself look good, even to himself. I hated his guts.

Then I heard the station wagon coming back again. They drove around to the back door and I heard the men tramping in and out of the house and setting things down. After that there were low-spoken directions, scuffing of feet and some bumping; the small slam of a screen door and the steady tread of the two through the hall as they carried Fargo up the rickety stairway I'd seen going from the hall to the second floor. They set what I supposed was the cot down directly above my head. There were some mumbled voices and the pair came back downstairs. I heard them back of me in the room. Pinky walked over and stood my chair on its legs. I watched him as he went around the kitchen table and sat down.

"All right, Joe, cut him loose." Joe came over and started to work behind the chair on my hands. I got sick from the cutting of the wire and tried not to vomit. The sweat dripped into my eyes and I couldn't get enough breath through my nose. Pinky came over and stripped the tape off my mouth with a jerk that damn near broke my neck. God! I'd have given a lot to have a clean smash at the guy on even terms.

My hands came free and I wanted to rub my wrists but I couldn't. Nothing would work. I could only hold them out in front of me and stare at them. Pinky said, "Get him a glass of water before you start on his feet." He said nothing while Joe got the glass. I didn't hear any water running. They probably had a well. When Joe got back, Pinky dumped the rest of the Forester in the water and gave it to me. I couldn't hold it and he poured it down me. I wanted to slap it out of his hand. But the drink helped.

The ankles weren't as bad. They hurt like hell but I didn't get sick any more. Finally Pinky said, "Can you walk?" I told him I supposed so and he told me to go upstairs and take a look at the kid.

I worked my wrists some and stood up. I sat right down again. Pinky sent Joe to the supplies for a bottle of whiskey and they gave me a big drink. After a while I stood up again and started for the hall. The pair of them bracketed me between them, Joe first and Pinky behind. I made it up without too much trouble.

Fargo was on a cot in a musty and extremely filthy bedroom. His bed linen was fresh, however, and he looked all right. He turned his eyes to me and said nothing. I asked him how he felt and he said, "Tired."

My stuff was piled on an old-fashioned bureau in the corner. The only light was a dirty globe suspended from the ceiling. I put the bag and a couple of boxes on the floor under the light and dug out what I needed to dress the kid's wound.

They'd apparently been careful with him. No evidence of fresh bleeding under my adhesive corset and the drains hadn't been noticeably disturbed. Nobody said anything until I'd finished the job. I didn't go into the subject of further care or feeding for the boy. The whole layout was too hopeless. The thing couldn't go on much longer this way. The pay-off had to be close. An air of desperate finality gripped the place and the people in it . . . the last, grim, dark refuge of the hunted; a hole with no way out except back again into the faces of the hunters.

I was looking among my things for a clean towel when Pinky sighed deeply and stood up. He turned to Joe.

"Go down to the station wagon and get me the big envelope that's in the glove compartment." Joe grunted and set off downstairs. Pinky paced slowly around the room while I found a clean towel and spread it on the bureau. I lay my bandage scissors and other stuff out carefully, waiting for something to happen. As Joe started to climb the stairs, Pinky hauled out his gun again and put it on the table in front of him. I knew it wasn't meant for me and said, "Is it that bad, Pinky?"

"Just that bad."

Joe walked into the room with his eyes on the gun. He handed the envelope to Pinky who put it into his breast pocket with his left hand without taking his eyes off the smaller man. Pinky watched him quietly until the guy began to shuffle his feet around. Then, in a voice that wouldn't have carried as far as the hall, he carved the following speech into Joe's heart:

"I want you to take the station wagon back, Joe, then I want to be rid of you for good. Shut up and listen! You stink of rottenness, outside and in. You lack the decencies of a mongrel dog and the loyalties of the commonest burglar. When you leave the car at the club, I want you to head out of town. You better get as far away as you can, Joe, because the first words I'm going to say to the cops when they bust in here will be your name . . . your name and your record. You'll do the rest of that time and be glad that somebody didn't kill you while you were out. Here's a hundred dollars. It's just twice as much as you got for selling me out to Lennen. Now get out!"

Joe got out. We sat in silence as he went. After the car had turned out of the yard, Pinky looked at me for the first time. He said:

"Cosy!"

"I don't think it's cosy." I wasn't in any mood for his guff and wasn't having any. "I think it stinks."

"What the hell do you suppose I think about it?" Pinky pulled out a pack of cigarettes and fumbled around for a match.

I dug into my pocket for a book and threw it on the table for him. It hurt my wrist and I wished I'd let him get his own match. I said, "I don't know *what* you'd think about it. How would I know? I've never bashed anybody over the head with a milk bottle."

Pinky's voice was gentle. I had never heard it so gentle. "I haven't either, Doc."

I got the terrible feeling that I was going to believe the son-of-a-bitch.

21

Pinky didn't amplify his statement. He just sat there and waited for me to say something. I said, "You've sure got Eddie Marsh fooled."

He took a long, thoughtful drag at his cigarette. "Eddie Marsh has a briefcase full of evidence that I can't argue with . . . yet."

"What do you mean, 'yet'?" There'd be no "yet" for the fellow when Marsh got him, and that would have to be soon. If Eddie had evidence of that kind against Pinky, there wouldn't be many holes in it. I said so.

"There aren't many holes in it. There's only one. There's always been only one." He stared at his feet. "Just that one . . . just that same, vague, torturing blank. It beat me once, seven years ago, and it's going to beat me this time. For good, this time." He shook his red head a couple of times. "Let's go downstairs, Doc. You all right, kid?"

Fargo looked at him. There was a wondering sympathy in his eyes that gave me the idea the boy didn't know all of it. "Sure. I'm in good shape . . . ain't I, Doc?" I told him he was okay . . . that I'd be back in a little while . . . and we went downstairs. Pinky walked behind, with his gun in his pocket. We sat down in the dirty parlor. I picked my wrist watch off the table where Joe had left it when he tied me. It said four o'clock. Two hours! What had happened to me in two hours shouldn't happen to a guy in a lifetime!

Pinky had shown symptoms of talking. Let him talk. My wrists reminded me that he wasn't going to do any talking that

would hurt him. They also reminded me that I was glad he
wasn't trying to make me do the talking.

Pinky threw his cigarette on the floor and scuffed at it with
his foot. "Yeah! One lousy human body . . . with a name I don't
know. One lousy human body with strength enough to bring a
milk bottle down on a man's head . . . with strength enough to
hit a half dead guy with a sap . . . or a club . . . or whatever he
used."

"Lennen was killed with a milk bottle as you know. Not a
club."

"Sam Kerschoff wasn't killed with a milk bottle. He was
killed with a blackjack or a soft club . . . or a foot."

"I don't understand . . . about Kerschoff, I mean."

"You don't have to. There's nothing you can do about it."

I said, "Okay." Kerschoff again. Eddie Marsh had said I was
in the hands of a convicted murderer . . . that he had beaten
a man to death. Pinky's telephone conversations about finding
some New York connection of Kerschoff's. The documents his
lawyer was to search . . . the papers Pinky had studied for seven
years. The fact that Pinky had said that the only man who knew
Kerschoff's New York connection was dead. Lennen, of course.

In other words, somebody Lennen knew was the key to
whatever problem was threatening Pinky. Pinky on five. The
telephone call at the place where there was music at eight-thirty
that night. Lennen had been there. Had the other man, if it
was a man, been there too? Lennen would have known him and
Pinky wouldn't.

If Pinky didn't actually know how this man Kerschoff had
been killed, he could hardly have killed him. It seemed pretty
evident that, if he hadn't killed Kerschoff, he must have been
accused of it . . . and, in the light of Eddie's warning to me,
convicted. Convicted, he must have done time. That made the
seven elapsed years since the event make sense.

So Pinky, looking for the killer of Kerschoff, free for seven
years, while an innocent man sweat it out in the pen, got too
close to the killer . . . through Lennen. Lennen promptly got
murdered.

I didn't try to place Fargo in the picture. Just took it for granted that he was tossed in there to make the thing more complicated. For some reason of Pinky's, Fargo was around where all these things were going on. I decided to forget him until the rest of the story straightened itself out.

Kerschoff had been killed with a sap . . . or a club . . . beaten to death with something. Or a foot. Kicked to death. Nasty thought. Savage, dirty way to die . . . or to kill. Both killings had the same feeling. Lennen's killer had pounded and pounded with that bottle on his victim's already crushed skull. They were . . . or were made, to seem . . . hysterical, unpremeditated attacks, insanely sponsored by some crashing rage or terror.

Yes, if my premise about Pinky was correct, neither killing had left enough evidence to lead to the *right* man and plenty of it to convict the *wrong* one. The big redhead, on that hypothesis, would have done six or seven years for one of the murders and couldn't safely face examination by the police on the other. It's a sound bet that no man can just up and beat two men to death and provide himself a fall guy in each instance without its catching up with him. It couldn't have been unpremeditated in at least one case. It had to be sly . . . sly and knowing and vicious.

It had to be a guy who knew all the risks and how to eliminate most of them. It had been odds-on that Lennen had to die, then, and his killer had made it odds-on that he wouldn't go to the chair for it.

Have I said, "he" all along? I guess you do that automatically when you talk about that sort of murder. Mrs. Frank Parrish-Lennen had been in a most advantageous spot if she had had any reason to get rid of her husband . . . the warmed-over lover who was brushing her off. Besides, there were ten thousand dollars under her hand . . . if she'd known where to find them . . . or had time. That, of course, is what she was looking for when she used the remaining milk bottle on me. I didn't think too much of Terry as a prospect for Eddie Marsh, but if he was damned fool enough to forget her, I wasn't going to be.

Finally I said, "Mind if I do some guessing?"

Pinky said, "What can I lose? I'll listen."

"Okay. This is all based on one viewpoint. For the moment, I'm going to believe that neither you nor the kid upstairs killed Lennen."

"That's right. But go ahead."

"I'm also going to believe, for the moment, that you didn't kill this Kerschoff." Pinky nodded. "Let's say you did time for manslaughter in connection with Kerschoff's killing."

"What makes you think that?" Sharply.

"I think that because you said you lost to this . . . this blank, name, body, whatever you call it . . . seven years ago. Also because Eddie Marsh said you were a convicted murderer."

The guy pounced like a terrier at a red ball. "When did he say that?"

My error. Well, hell. "On Katie's broadcast." I had to grin.

"I'll be damned!" He looked genuinely surprised. "All right. Now tell me how you heard it."

"You have a ventilator shaft from the office to the bathroom upstairs in the other house."

Pinky gave the whole thing a double take, thought it over, started to laugh, stopped quick and said, "What else did you hear?" Then, "Never mind, go ahead with your guessing."

"Well, I figure you did time for Kerschoff's death. I won't try to guess the circumstances, but it must have been a brawl or the charge would have been a tougher rap. I think you've been looking for the guy that killed Kerschoff ever since you got out. Maybe you're on parole from someplace . . . you probably are, if the other thing is true."

Pinky didn't move a muscle as I looked up at him. When I stared off at the wall again I heard him light a cigarette. "Lennen knew, somehow, who the guy is and you had made some sort of a deal with him. Maybe a ten grand deal. Somebody had, that's sure. Before you can complete the deal and find the man you're after, Lennen is killed. You were close by . . . close enough so that Marsh has you pegged for the murder. I can't guess where Fargo fits in or how he got shot."

"Why you doing all this guessing, Doc?"

"Partly curiosity. Partly the fact that I'm in bad with Marsh
. . . maybe in more trouble than he can handle for me . . ."

Pinky didn't say anything.

"There's another reason why I'm doing all this guessing. If
I'm ever to get in the clear with Eddie Marsh, I've got to come
up with the right answer. If you didn't kill Lennen, I may get
the right answer from you."

"What's the use of all that, Doc. I didn't kill Lennen and I
don't know the right answer." He got up and began that damned
pacing of his again. I knew I was getting someplace. I didn't
know where, but he was going to tell me something that would
make sense. I said:

"I think you have the answer and don't know it."

He wheeled on me. "How? . . . *How?*" Pinky sat down suddenly. "How, for the love of God? The thing's had me nuts for
years. Your guesses were right on the nose, Doc. All except the
ten grand. I can't understand that angle. The rest is right. In
all these years there has been only one lousy clue to the guy
who killed Kerschoff and sent me up. One lousy clue to place
anybody at the scene after I'd left it . . . a clue that was so silly
that the prosecuting attorney got a laugh out of the jury when
he spoke of it in his summation! I did six years because nobody
would believe a witness who said he'd heard somebody sneeze in
the tack-room after I'd left it!"

The bells in the back of my mind sounded like New Year's
Eve. I hollered so loud that he jumped. "Somebody did *what?
Where?!*"

"I had a witness who could swear to the fact that I left . . ."

I hollered again. "Shut up, goddammit, and tell me what I
want to know! You said somebody sneezed in a tack-room?"

"Yes. Nothing more than that. It definitely proved . . ."

"Hold it! Listen! I've got something and I'm going to follow
it up. Through that ventilator I heard a remark you made to your
lawyer implying that Fargo could identify this guy. Can he?"

"He thinks so. Maybe he can and probably Terry Hale . . ."

"Terry Hale could identify him?" Brother! This thing began
to pile up on me!

"I'm pretty sure she could." He'd caught the fever, but he was tense and wary. "Now that she's turned up as Lennen's wife."

"Would this guy know she could?" I asked. "The killer?"

"I think so. Maybe not. It was a long time ago. You see . . ."

"Would the murderer *think* she could identify him . . . *after* he found out she was Lennen's wife?"

"I think so. Yes, probably. The trouble is . . ."

"Listen, Pinky! There's no time to talk. Let's get going!" I jumped up and started for the door with only one idea in mind. Pinky's step slammed after me. I felt my shoulder yanked from behind and spun around to look at the muzzle of that gun again.

"Not so fast. What the hell is this?"

"If you didn't kill Kerschoff and Lennen, come on with me. I'm taking you and all the cops in New York County to the guy that did. Make up your mind fast. If you killed them, we'll forget it. If you didn't, shake the lead out and drive me to a telephone!" He hesitated an instant and I added, "Goddammit, I'm believing you . . . you can believe me for a while!"

He put up his gun. "Okay, Doc. I hope you know what you're doing. It won't be nice for me out there if you don't."

"I know what I'm doing. I'll go alone if you want. I took it for granted you wouldn't let me."

"All right. I'm ready." He glanced upstairs as we hit the hall. "The kid be all right?" I told him the kid would be in a decent hospital by daylight. I called up to the boy, "Sit tight, Fargo, the boss and I are going on an errand." We heard his "Okay" as we closed the front door.

We were bouncing out of the lane when Pinky said, "Where to?" I told him I wanted that telephone first and he started back toward the club. He drove like an old-time bootlegger and hit those macadam corners like a bat out of hell. The joint was dark when we pulled down the drive. A sign on the road read, "The Poplars" . . . beneath that, it said, ". . . a poplar place to dine and dance." That's what it said. I know. I went back yesterday to check it and eat a steak. The poplar place to dine and dance was dark, except for a mournful light in the kitchen. We pounded across the porch and into a side door. One turn in the dim reflection of the kitchen light and we were at the office. Pinky lighted the lights and indicated the telephone. As I went to pick up the instrument, his big hand closed over mine. It was wet. Maybe you think mine wasn't!

"Keep this right, Doc. I'm in a tough spot and . . . well, keep it right, that's all."

I got the operator and called Police Headquarters, Manhattan. Pinky was nervous and suspicious when I asked him to write down the address of the farmhouse. But he did it while I was getting Eddie's home number.

Marsh was bright as midday when he answered. "Marsh," he said. I told him who it was and he started a tirade that he must have been rehearsing for days. I told him to shut up and listen.

"I'm going to get your Lennen killer for you . . ."

"Jackson! My God, Doc! Where? Listen, you! Stay away . . ."

I shut him off again. "I don't know who Jackson is but . . ."

At my elbow, I heard Pinky say, "I'm Jackson, Doc." On the phone I heard Eddie say, "Pinky Jackson, the Chicago bookmaker. He's a convicted murderer. He's damned dangerous. Did you hear my broadcast?"

"Yes, I heard it. You were wonderful. Why don't you make a career out of it?"

I had to holler, that time, to stop his swearing. "I'm telling *you* it's important. You're not telling *me*. Listen. Get your clothes on and get some cops and a car out to where you are now and hold 'em there. Then send an ambulance to a white farmhouse set back from the road about three hundred feet north of the intersection of Swamp Road and Fenster Road near Parkstown, Long Island. Got that?" He repeated the directions and asked if they'd need a squad car. "No. There's a sick boy on the second floor. Tell them to handle him carefully and take him to a hospital. I'll call you back."

"But Jackson . . ."

"Jackson is sitting here beside me. You don't want him."

"The hell I don't! Listen, Doc . . ."

"Quiet! Do what I tell you. I can't take time to explain. Don't bother to trace this call. It isn't important and we're leaving. I'll call you."

He was roaring something when I hung up.

I called Terry Hale's hotel. "Out," the night man said. I called information and got all the numbers I could collect for Empire City Racetrack and kept calling them until I got a watchman. Yes, he could give me Sam Eckman's number where he lived but I'd have to wait. I waited. A small hotel in the Bronx. When Sam answered, I said:

"This is Doc Connor, Sam. Where's Terry . . . Gladys?"

"Gladys? I don't know, Doc. What's wrong? Has something happened to her?"

"I'm afraid she may be in danger, Sam . . . maybe not . . . but I want to find her. She's not at her hotel."

Sam said, "My God, Doc, that's terrible. She might have stayed with her girl friend. She does, sometimes." I asked him who the girl friend was and he remembered . . . a Nancy Tierney and she lived at the Belford Apartments in Eighty-sixth Street. Her number was listed.

I woke Nancy up and she yawned in my ear. She said who was I when I asked about Terry Hale. I said I was the Police Department and that Hale was in danger.

"She knew that, mister. I tried to get her to go to the cops but she was scared on account of they had her in the can so . . ."

"All right, where is she? Quick. We've got to get to her."

"Where'd you get my number?"

"She gave us your name as a friend. Here at Headquarters."

"I know. The cops checked me. I guess you must be okay. Yes. I'll tell you where she is and why. Last night somebody tried to get into her room from the fire escape. Her room at the hotel. She ran out in the hall and made a fuss and he got away. She didn't call the cops because she was scared of him. She told people around that she'd had a nightmare. Then she . . ."

"Where the hell is she? The same guy will kill her this time if he finds her!"

"She's gone over to another girl's apartment . . . a girl who came to see her when she was in jail. She said she'd be safe there."

"What's the girl's name?"

"She didn't tell me. She just said she'd be safe there."

"I hope so. You don't know anything more about it, then?"

"No." I thanked her and hung up. I called Marsh back and told him to get a lot of men on Terry and see if they could locate her and that I was on the way into town as fast as I could get there. He said a lot of things I was sure he'd regret later, but among them I heard him say he was leaving the place and for me to keep in touch with radio through the Headquarters board. That made sense. I might not have thought of it. I could catch him whenever we got to town.

About seven, I'd call Katie and tell her I was all right. She didn't have a show on Saturdays and Sundays and would sleep late. Pinky said, "Well, how about it, Doc?" I told him we'd drive to New York and clean it all up with Marsh. He seemed puzzled and hesitant.

"I don't like it. I know the case the New York cops have against me. As far as they're concerned . . . as far as a jury would be concerned, for that matter . . . it's foolproof. I haven't the slimmest lead to the guy the cops ought to be looking for instead of me."

"I have."

"You have what?"

"The slimmest lead. Slim as that picture wire your guy Joe tied me with. But it will hold. It'll hang him. You do still hang 'em in Illinois, don't you?"

Pinky shuddered and didn't even bother to say no.

22

As we headed for New York, a vague, gray halation struggled with the eastern gloom behind us and the million lights of the City made only a cloud-sodden glow against the morning mist. A chilling drizzle sucked in at the windows.

Pinky drove fast and well. I was interested in learning that my bookmaker friend from Chicago . . . after seven years out of circulation . . . knew Long Island like an umpire knows a baseball diamond.

We'd been going along a while when he spoke. "I don't know what the hell I'm running into, Doc, but I've got to the point where nothing I can do gets me any further. We weren't good for twenty-four hours longer at the old farm and I knew it. I had no place else to go."

"The cops would have looked for you at the farm?"

"The cops had looked for me at the farm. I found their tracks and figured they wouldn't come back for a while. The Poplars belongs to a friend in New York . . . a bookmaker. I couldn't afford to get him into trouble when they took out after me."

"I see." Then an idea hit me. "The friend, the bookmaker, where you were the night Lennen was killed?"

"How did you know? . . . But you told me. Terry Hale heard somebody holler 'Pinky.'"

"That's right. Tell me. I thought it must have been a book-maker's office but I couldn't figure out two things. One of them was why four lines would be busy at eight-thirty in the evening, and the other is why there was music playing. Terry said there was a juke-box or a radio or something going on in the background."

"That's simple enough. Hollywood Park was running. Eight-thirty here is five-thirty on the Coast. The races were over but they would have been checking mutuel-payoffs for the day before closing the wire."

"For a guy that's followed racing as long as I have, I'm pretty stupid. I never should have given that one a second thought!" Dull!

"I damned well hope you're not being stupid now!"

"I'm not being stupid this time. But how about the juke-box?"

"It was a radio. The Coast wire is open for a couple of hours after everything else is dead. A bunch of guys who have handled five or six tracks all afternoon get jumpy when there's nothing going on. They play the radio. It isn't a customer place. It's a good sized lay-off book. It's a clearing house for a couple of dozen smaller books."

That made sense. Lennen, as a small time hanger-on and occasional runner for a book, could have been around there and they probably would let him use a telephone. We drove on a minute or two and Pinky, staring straight ahead at the road, started to talk.

"This bookmaker and I were boys together. His folks lived in the house where The Poplars is now, and I lived . . . back there where Fargo is. That was my home for years and the cops had to find it out sooner or later."

No wonder he knew Long Island. I said nothing.

"I was fascinated by horse-races as a kid and drifted around the Long Island tracks most of my spare time. I liked the horses and the training and the riding. Gambling never appealed to me. I learned very early in life that there were only two kinds of horse-players . . . the guy who had a lot of fun and took winnings and losses alike . . . as they came . . . and the chump."

". . . and the percentage boys, of course."

"Naturally. Where there are a lot of chumps and careless players, you're bound to find some percentage guys. As you know, they're comparatively few and far between." He thought a moment. "As I grew older I saw that the only fellow who made any money from all this betting was the bookmaker . . . the guy who pays track prices and doesn't have to give up the take . . . the dough that otherwise is taken out by the track and for taxes. It's illegal, naturally, but usually winked at and used for petty political grafting.

"So I worked my way up from a little handbook around New York to quite a big layout in Chicago. I say big . . . it was a good-sized book for one man to bank and operate. Most of the time I contented myself with the sure profit . . . with the percentage. Any time I got too much on a horse, I'd lay it off to a bigger book . . . almost always, it would be with this friend in New York where Terry Hale heard the music.

"Well, one day, seven years ago, a small bookmaker around Chicago came to me and asked me if I wanted to handle part of a big sucker bet. His name was Kerschoff and all I knew about him was that he had been around a long time and hadn't been in any trouble. I asked him about this bet and he said that a New York millionaire wanted to place a big bet on a jumping race in Maryland. He said the horse would be around third favorite against a three-time winner named "Turret" who didn't look like he could lose.

"I asked Kerschoff who was placing the bet and he told me it was the owner of the horse . . . a man named Walters . . . but that he didn't want it known and was betting through a commissioner.

"I told Kerschoff I'd let him know at his hotel that night and got rid of him. I wanted the bet, of course. But I wanted to check on it. I called my New York connection and asked him what he knew. He said he had heard of the bet but hadn't seen any of the money. He figured they thought they could keep it away from the Maryland track by placing the money in Chicago to keep from spoiling the price, of course. He made a quick line for me. Only three contention horses. The favorite, 'Knighthood'—6/5 . . . some other horse . . . I forget his name, at 3/1 and 'Turret'—5/1. He didn't seem to see anything wrong with the bet and I took it . . . a lot of it. I made a small commission deal with Kerschoff and spent the next few hours wondering how much of it to hold and, in general, worrying about the whole thing.

"Then I got a call from the New York book. My friend. He said the bet smelled; that the owner of 'Turret' had turned up at one of the books he dealt with and bet a thousand on the horse to place. To place, for God's sake, and I was holding ten grand on the horse that he was supposed to have bet to win! On the surface it might look like 'Turret' didn't have much chance and that my bet was safe. I didn't kid myself. Maybe his owner thought 'Turret' was only as good as second, but *somebody* in New York knew 'Turret' was going to win. I asked the bookmaker where the money had come from and he said he couldn't find out but that he'd heard it was some New York sharpshooter.

"I tried to lay off some of that bet every place I could think of. At five to one, the bet would break me. But everybody in the trade was afraid of it by that time. I was stuck with it. I was the sucker. Kerschoff was in partnership with some out-of-town sharpshooter and the race was fixed.

"As far as the bet is concerned, you can guess the rest. Lennen rode the favorite, 'Knighthood,' as Mr. Parrish, and damned near killed himself making it look good. I went for the works, but I had no choice. I closed up.

"Then things began to get around. Some stableboy had heard the fix arranged with Parrish. At least that was the rumor. You may remember that there was sort of an investigation, but nobody could be convinced that a boy would risk an injury of that sort to throw a race. It was dropped and I had to take the beating. I had delayed the payoff until the inquiry was over and then, one day, met Kerschoff at the track to give him the dough.

"We went over to the stable area and into Art Merrick's tack-room. Art wasn't there. It was late afternoon after the races and the place was deserted except for the watchmen.

"I told Kerschoff what I thought of him and gave him the dough. Every damned cent I could raise. Every cent I had put together since I'd been making book. I watched him stuff it in his breast pocket and went off my nut. He was a big guy. I called him a name and he laughed at me. I hit him. He hit me a couple of times and I took him. I hit him a lot, and hard . . . but he was just out when I left him. I broke my hands on his head but I couldn't have killed him.

"As I walked out of the tack-room and around the corner of the barn, I saw a watchman standing across the road with his back to me. He turned at my step. He knew me and wanted to chat about my cut face. I told him I'd had a fight with a guy and walked away.

"The watchman got curious after standing there a minute or two, and went into the Merrick barn to investigate. You can guess the answer to that, too. Kerschoff was dead and the dough was gone. The money I'd given him and seen him pocket. As the watchman started off to call the police, he heard someone sneeze back of him in the barn. He thought he saw a man going around the corner of the next barn as he went back to find out who sneezed. That's all. He was a lousy witness."

Pinky drove on in silence while I digested all this with increasing enthusiasm. It fit. It worked with the things I thought and the things I knew. I said, "Then you were convicted of manslaughter and served . . . what? Six years?"

"Six out of ten. The war years. They weren't pleasant, pal. They were hell to do without letting myself go completely sour. God knows I had plenty opportunity to get bitter. But there was a guy there who helped me some . . . a lifer with a lot of privileges and a job as librarian. He was the man who got hold of Fargo for me. Fargo'd just gotten out of the service and was looking for a job with the horses. He heard about my case, and the talk of the race that had come up at the trial and happened to remark that he knew the race had been fixed because he heard it fixed. Fargo was the stableboy of the rumor. The racing commission hadn't heard about him and he hadn't been questioned. He wrote a letter to the authorities at Joliet and, while it wouldn't have any bearing on my sentence, which had almost run out, they gave it to me. I talked to the librarian about it and he got in touch with the kid. When I got out, I came to

New York and looked him up. Fargo said he could recognize the man who had set up the fix and we started out looking for him. It was tough. We haunted every book in town . . . every gambling place we could find. We asked questions . . . too many, I guess, because it got around that I was out and looking for the man who'd broken me. Only the guy, himself, knew I was looking for the man who'd also double-crossed, robbed and killed his own partner in the deal.

"Among the people who heard about it was Parrish . . . Lennen. Joe told him and got fifty bucks for it. Lennen didn't know me, of course, because he'd never seen me . . . nor I him. Fargo saw him on the street one day and recognized him as the jockey in the fix. He followed him to my friend's bookmaking office, but lost him, later, when he left. I took to hanging around there.

"Then, one night, while I was waiting there, I got a call from the kid . . . that was the night Lennen was killed . . ."

The Pinky on five call! This thing was really adding up!

". . . telling me that Lennen was in the same room with me. He'd seen him come in. Fargo described him and I looked around. Lennen was at one of the other phones."

I broke in. "Telling Terry Hale he was in a fair way to get hold of a lot of dough and that he loved her. And asking her to meet him right away. I'll say he was in a fair way to get some dough! He undoubtedly had ten thousand dollars on him!"

"I can't make that out."

"I think I can . . . but go on with the story. It's holding together perfectly."

"I got a good look at Lennen and let him go out without following him. After he'd stepped out the door, I asked one of the boys who he was. I didn't get much . . . just a chiseler around, maybe ran a small book, never bothered anybody. Name of Harry Lennen. Lived up in Fifty-third, near Seventh Avenue.

"I figured Fargo would follow the guy, so I waited a while, then wandered up in that direction. I was walking through Fifty-third when I found Fargo. He was stooped over, leaning against an alley wall next to a brick apartment building. He had been shot. I asked him who did it and he didn't know. He managed to say something about Lennen . . . second floor this building . . . and I ran up there. You know what I saw. I had to pull Fargo back in the shadow and get my car. I thought nobody saw us . . . but somebody did, from what Eddie Marsh says."

I asked him what Fargo had run into.

"Fargo followed Lennen away from the bookmakers and watched him go into the house. In a minute or two, he . . . damned fool kid . . . sneaked into the hall, went up to the second story and opened the door. The lights were out in the room but the hall light showed somebody moving around in there. He said, 'Hey, Mr. Parrish!' He said there wasn't a sound for a few seconds, then somebody shot him in the belly."

"But that can't be. With the door open that shot would have brought people around. Someone would have heard it. Nobody heard anything."

"The gun had a silencer. I picked it up. It's been my ace in the hole. The guy who killed Lennen smashed past the kid and out the door. Fargo, even with a slug in his guts, grabbed the fellow's arm and caught the barrel and the silencer. The killer must have been in a panic because he dropped the gun."

"And didn't come back for it."

Pinky looked up from his driving. "How do you know?"

"It couldn't have been the killer's gun. He'd have come back. He had time. It had to be Lennen's gun. The murderer must have found it while looking for . . . something else."

"Ten thousand dollars."

"That's right." We drove on a minute. I asked Pinky how Fargo could have made it down the stairs without leaving bloodstains.

"I don't know. He said he couldn't walk but he'd crawled down on his good side and his fanny. That might have had something to do with it. But that was the whole story. I got the kid into the car and took him to the club. That's all of it."

I didn't need much more. I had the thing wrapped up and myself pretty well cleared of trouble. At least I could come up with the right guy and make it pretty tough for Eddie to squawk

about the suppression of evidence and the obstruction of jus-
tice. Hell, I was the possessor of the only real evidence and the
defender of the oppressed. I felt great. I'd wake up Katie. It was
almost six and we were only a mile or so from the Queensbor-
ough Bridge. I spotted a place where we could have coffee and
I could phone. Pinky said okay and we stopped. It was murky
and wet out. The lights looked welcome.

We picked up a couple of cups of coffee and some doughnuts
and I beat it for a phone, taking a doughnut with me. I dialed
and heard Katie's phone ring . . . once. She answered before the
second ring.

"What are you doing up so early . . . or have you had a . . ."

"Jimmy! Oh Jimmy, where are you?" Wait a minute! She was
off key. The words were right for the royal welcome but the
tone was very wrong.

"What's the matter, darling?"

"I don't know, Jimmy. I'm afraid! Terry Hale's here and . . ."

"How the hell did she get there. Say! What goes on?"

"I went to see her in jail . . . I wondered if I could find some
lead to you. She called me tonight and said somebody tried to
get into her room at the hotel."

"I know about that. Go on. Quick!" I dropped my doughnut.

"She thinks someone followed her here. She was sure of it
but I talked her out of it. Now she's asleep, but I'm certain
there's somebody out on the kitchen fire escape. I'm scared . . ."

"Goddammit, call the cops! Call Headquarters! Ask radio
to get Eddie Marsh. I'll be there in three minutes." I slammed
across the joint, hollering to Pinky on the way out. We hit that
car together and the red-head landed in the driver's seat. He
drove like a 1929 bootlegger.

By the time we screamed into the bridge approach, made the
turn with rubber howling like a banshee, we had a siren on our
tail.

God bless the siren! Let him come!

23

We roared into Katie's street and skidded to the curb. We had agreed that I was to go in the front way and Pinky was to take the back. The apartment was on the back corner of the fourth floor, giving the whole side an exposure to the East and the river.

There was an alley running between Katie's building and the next one and Pinky ducked down it. The speed cop parked and went after him. I ran in the front way and found the night man still on. I said, "Come on . . . bring your pass keys . . . there's trouble." He wasn't a young man, but he moved fast. We were on our way up when I heard sirens and knew that the building would be surrounded in a matter of sixty seconds.

Just as I jumped through the elevator door at the fourth floor, Katie burst out of her apartment and flew toward me down the hall. I passed her on the run and she screamed, "No. No, Jimmy, no! He's in the kitchen. He's got a gun!"

That slowed me up and I ran to the side of the half open door and plastered myself to the wall. A shot wasped by my face and I yelled to Katie and the nightman to get into the elevator and go down. They made it close as another slug snarled by. I was nailed to that wall for the duration . . . no gun, no shelter. I couldn't reach the door to lock the guy in. I waited for another shot. If he'd heard me tell Katie to go down in the elevator, he knew he didn't stand a chance through the hall. He'd have to go back to the fire escape.

Then I heard his feet pounding through the apartment . . .
away from me. I jumped in and saw his broad, fat back as he
ran toward the kitchen. I got as far as the kitchen door before
he wheeled and snapped another shot at me. I saw him turn,
jumped to the side of the door and heard one of Katie's pictures
behind me explode in a thundering crash.

I couldn't see him any more but I heard him scream. I've
heard guys scream before, in case you don't believe they do.
This guy didn't scream because he was hurt. He screamed because he saw death staring him straight in the face . . . straight
in his fat, rotten, sweating face.

I stepped into the doorway in time to see it all. Jocko Burns
was crouched in the middle of the kitchen staring at the window on the fire escape. Pinky was half way in the window, his
gun blazing brilliant orange blobs. I dropped to the floor and
crawled sideways out of the line of fire.

I didn't need to. The slugs were ripping through Burns and
stopping there. He started spinning back with the impact and
fell heavily to the floor. Pinky leaned back to yell something
below and I jumped to get Burns' gun.

He was on his side, propped on one elbow with the gun in
his free hand. I was half way across the floor to him when he
shot. With his last, nasty breath he screamed again and with the
last movement of his nasty body, he pulled the trigger. For the
first time in his rotten sure-thing life he played a hundred-to-
one shot and it paid off.

I saw Pinky for a moment, well back on the fire escape, reel-
ing farther backward. In a great shouting voice he said:

"Oh . . . God . . . NO!"

They say he didn't say anything else on the way from the
rail to the ground. I hope he was dead when he hit. Of course
I know he wasn't.

I hauled myself up and turned around toward some noise behind me. The hall was full of cops . . . piling into the apartment
like a Keystone comedy in the days when comedies were funny.
I put my hand to my face because something burned me there
and found a lot of blood. I couldn't figure what had happened. I

turned again and Eddie Marsh was jumping through the kitchen window. He said, "Doc! Are you okay?"

I said I was okay and there's the guy on the floor and he'd better look in the bedroom for Terry Hale. I followed him in and we found her sitting on the bed, unharmed. She was shaking a little, but in good control of herself. Eddie asked her if she was hurt.

"No. I'm all right. What about Jocko?"

Eddie Marsh said, "Who?"

I said, "Your killer, Eddie." Then, "He's dead, Terry."

"Thank God! He's tried to kill me twice tonight. It's been pretty terrible . . . I . . ." She started to cry and I knew it was all over. I turned around and ran straight into a wild-eyed, onrushing Katie. She hugged me and got blood on herself and said a lot of nice things about oh-jimmy-darling-so-afraid-for-me-what-had-I-done-to-my-face and promptly sat down beside Terry and blubbered. They put their arms around each other and cried a tuneless duet. Nobody paid any attention to me at all. Damned if I can understand women.

Eddie Marsh called me into the kitchen and said, "This fellow, they tell me, is Jocko Burns. What makes you think he killed Lennen? We've never even talked with him."

"Have your people picked up the boy that was shot?"

"Yes. We got him an hour ago. He's in the hospital. Why?"

"This fellow shot him the night he killed Lennen. The gun's around. It probably will have prints on it. Maybe not. He also killed a guy named Kerschoff in Chicago."

"Jackson killed Kerschoff. Did time for it."

"It doesn't make much difference, does it? Pinky Jackson's out in the alley. Is he dead?" Eddie said he was. I said, "The poor bastard!"

"Did you see them both shot?" I told Eddie I had and he busied himself with Burns' pockets. Over his shoulder, he said, "I suppose you can straighten this thing out someway. You'd damned well better! I'll get the routine under way and see you later."

I went back to find out how the gals were faring and discovered them dabbing at their faces. Katie kissed me nicely and took me out to the bathroom to dab mine. I had a mean-looking gouge from a bullet. When or how I got it remains a mystery. I settled for believing it was a ricochet of one of Pinky's shots off some of Burns' bony structure. Anyway, it was messy enough to keep Katie occupied for a very pleasant few minutes and to give me what promises to be a distinguished dueling scar . . . a la Heidelberg.

The cops were milling around all over the place, so, while Katie was straightening up in the bathroom I went in to see how Terry was getting along. I said, "How is it going, Mrs. Parrish?" She flared up.

"Don't call me that, Doc. If you know as much about this thing as you sound like you do, you know how terribly I hate that name! He was a heel. He always was a heel."

"How much does Marsh know about the . . . the second milk bottle? I thought he had you on that." I grinned at her and she grinned back.

"They had some arguments among themselves in the Department Laboratory about the so-called hair and bloodstains. There wasn't enough hair to be important and it wasn't Lennen's anyway. As for the bloodstains, they were, in total, hardly enough to test . . . and they think the blood wasn't his either."

I grinned again and said I was fascinated, please go on.

"I told them I nearly always straightened up my estranged husband's apartment and they'd find my fingerprints on practically everything in the place. They found plenty, at that. When nothing else seemed to fit, they forgot about the bottle. Then, when they settled on Jackson, they let me go."

"What were you looking for that night, Terry?"

"Can't you guess?"

"I'd taken it for granted it was the money . . . but, with what I've learned since, I don't think you knew about that."

"I didn't." Terry sat down suddenly on the edge of the bed. "I was looking for the one thing I couldn't let you . . . or *anybody* find out about. Not as much for me as for my father. It was the one thing which could have connected us up with all this . . .

my wedding certificate. Harry had always used it as sort of a club over me."

"I see." Of course. ". . . and over Sam Eckman?"

"Indirectly, yes. Although the only crooked thing that ever happened in our barn . . . it was ours, then . . . Harry pulled alone."

I told her I could believe that and said, "Okay, kid, I'll forgive you. What's a tap on the head between friends?"

"Thanks, Doc."

"One more thing, Terry. Are you sure you didn't see Jocko Burns at any time during that evening?"

"Absolutely. I'd have said so. Why?"

"I keep wondering what the hell he was doing between the time he killed Lennen and turned up at my place. He had almost half an hour."

Terry said, "Jocko? Hell, Doc, he was probably back at that office of his figuring out the odds on his getting away with it!"

Through the door I watched a couple of guys in white coats struggling out with a long basketful of that dead pig. I made my way through the kitchen and looked down into the courtyard. Two cops were standing there talking. They'd taken Pinky away, too.

Eddie Marsh walked in and said he was sending Terry home with one of his men and asked me if I wanted to stick around a while. I said I didn't want to stay very long. He assured me he just needed enough to report and then he could get busy on the clean-up. I told him okay and found Katie. She was hauling out a bottle of Forester which she kept around for me.

The two of us had a drink together and got some of those gentle mutterings out of our systems. They'd look like hell on paper because they didn't make the sort of sense you can understand when you're reading a book. The place was quieting down steadily and finally Eddie came in, after knocking politely, and dropped into a chair.

"I wish to hell you'd leave the police business to the police, Doc."

"Right now I think it's a hell of an idea. You can have it."

"Will you tell me the story once over light . . . details later?"

"Actually, Eddie, you can use the story any way you like it. The man you thought killed Lennen . . . and had a beautiful case against . . . is on his way downtown in a basket. The man I *know* killed him, is also on his way downtown in a basket."

"The man you *know* killed Lennen! You'll really have to have something, Doc." Eddie was ready to argue. I wasn't.

"Listen, Eddie, I'm pooped and I want to get this over with. You've got a slug that I took out of a boy's belly. Someplace in Pinky Jackson's effects you'll find a gun with a silencer on it. They'll match. Ten to one the gun'll have Burns' prints on it . . . maybe not. It won't make any difference anyway, because the boy caught Jocko in Lennen's apartment before Lennen had stopped breathing."

"That close!"

"That close. The boy, Fargo, watched Lennen walk into the house and stood there at the door until he, himself, followed Lennen up. Nobody else went in. Burns had to be waiting there."

"If there aren't any prints on the gun can the boy identify Burns?"

"No. But I'm pretty sure I can tell you who can."

"Who?"

"Sam Eckman."

"Sam Eckman! That doesn't make sense! We've talked with Eckman and he doesn't turn up importantly anywhere in the case." Eddie was about to throw out everything I'd said.

"Well, one place Sam Eckman *did* turn up importantly in the case, Eddie, was at Lennen's front door at around nine-five that night. I think, if you question him, now that everything is wound up and his daughter is well out of it, you'll find that he'll tell you several things you didn't know."

"Such as?"

"Such as verifying Pinky's story about finding Fargo wounded in the alley and taking him away. You see, Sam was in front of the building . . . and *leaving* the neighborhood . . . at ten minutes after nine. Terry saw him. I don't believe he saw her or he'd have said something to her."

"That fits"

"Fits what?" I was curious at once. "Have you got anything that fits with Eckman?"

"Not until just now." Eddie looked uneasy. "When you were being held I took a chance on putting out a statement that we had definitely placed Pinky Jackson at the scene."

"Took a chance . . . you?"

"I got a note . . . a personal note . . . saying that the writer had seen Jackson at Lennen's place at nine-five. It said that, if the testimony were needed, he'd come in and give it."

"That's all? You couldn't trace it?"

"No. Now I see it had to be Eckman."

I felt a bit set up. "He was there."

"And you figure he'd been there for some time?"

"Yes. So much so that he was my first suspect for the killing. I went out to talk to him about it and he got tough. Warned me. Now I know it was his trainer's license he was thinking about . . . his reputation on the track. He'd heard the talk around town, I think, and went over to Lennen's to warn him in the same way. When he got there he saw Burns come out in a hurry, recognized him and stepped back into the shadows. That would be a couple of minutes after nine. Then I think he saw Fargo stumble out and, a minute later, saw Pinky turn up. He must have seen them drive off because he was walking away when Terry appeared at nine-ten."

"Think he saw her?"

"Absolutely not. Knowing there was something wrong, he would have turned up at Headquarters the minute you arrested her. If he'd *seen* Terry, he would have been able to provide her with some sort of an alibi."

Eddie puzzled quietly for a while. Katie came over and sat on the arm of my chair. I was pretty punchy and wished like hell to be let alone . . . not by Katie. Pretty soon Eddie said, "You figure Lennen had shaken Jocko Burns down for the ten grand, don't you?"

"Both of them are dead so my guess is as good as yours. I figure Lennen convinced Burns that Pinky was either going to get his dough back . . . or leave Jocko lying around someplace in the same condition he'd left Kerschoff. Then Burns let Lennen act as a go-between. Jocko wasn't afraid of Lennen, but he was terrified of Pinky. He thought Lennen was too small-time to cross him in a big deal . . . especially if there were a couple of hundred extra in it."

"Yes, that could be the way it was." Eddie got up and rummaged around for his hat. "I guess I've got enough if it checks. There are a lot of things I *could* ask, Doc, but I can't see the need for them now. Maybe they're better left out."

Maybe they were. It didn't make much difference. The whole, damned rotten mess didn't make any difference. Marsh had his case . . . and one to spare. I'd lost a guy I'd like to have had for a friend . . . a guy I'd liked to have helped win a bet. But he was predestined to be a loser.

Katie's arms were around me. She said, "Eddie, I'm taking this guy home, throwing him into a hot tub, putting him to bed and getting his breakfast. Why don't you run along and play with your other little policemen?"

Eddie sighed and said, "He's your problem, Katie." The big lug just stood there with his face hanging out until I said, "Well, what the hell you waiting around for? You heard the lady!"

He grinned like a kid and said, "I was just thinking what the good folks around Forty-eighth and Broadway will think when they hear that this sort of thing goes on over here in Beekman Place."

Katie said, "Goddammit, Eddie, go home!"

I poured another drink as Katie watched Eddie to the door. My sore wrists hurt like hell and I had pictures of the big redhead standing over me, watching Joe wire me up. Pictures of his hard face when he kicked my chair over on the floor. Pictures of his last terrible protest against the way fate treats a loser . . . "Oh . . . God . . . NO!"

"Pinky on five!"

Katie said, "What, darling?"

Print-on-demand titles available at
CoachwhipBooks.com

Ebook titles available at
Coachwhip.com

murder is mutuel

JACK DOLPH

Jack Dolph

MURDER MAKES THE MARE GO

hot tip JACK DOLPH

TIP SHEET
DAILY RATINGS

JACK DOLPH

DEAD ANGEL

A.M. JAUSS

TYLINE PERRY

THE OWNER
LIES DEAD

FRANCIS WALLACE

Little
HERCULES

A *Detective Novel* CLASSIC

A FULL LENGTH NOVEL

MEDORA
FIELD

WHO KILLED
AUNT MAGGIE?

BLOOD ON HER SHOE

MEDORA FIELD

THE CAT
SCREAMS
A HUGH RENNERT MYSTERY

TODD DOWNING

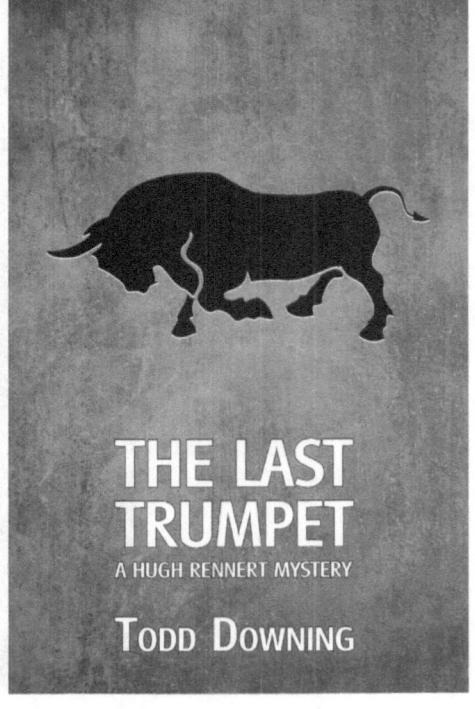

THE LAST
TRUMPET
A HUGH RENNERT MYSTERY

TODD DOWNING

NIGHT OVER
MEXICO
A HUGH RENNERT MYSTERY

TODD DOWNING

THE CASE OF THE
UNCONQUERED
SISTERS
A HUGH RENNERT MYSTERY
TODD DOWNING

HIDE AND GO SEEK

with, GOING TO ST. IVES

HOTEL

COLVER HARRIS

THE HOUSE THAT JACK BUILT

with, MURDER IN AMBER

COLVER HARRIS

THE
THING
IN THE
BRO⃝K

PETER STORME

LAVERNE RICE
WELL DRESSED
FOR MURDER

DETECTIVES 4

MISS MADELYN MACK
HUGH C. WEIR

MISS VAN SNOOP
CLARENCE ROOK

VIOLET STRANGE
ANNA KATHARINE GREEN

FLORENCE CUSACK
MEADE & EUSTACE

DETECTIVES 2

LOVEDAY BROOKE
CATHERINE LOUISA PIRKIN

LADY MOLLY OF SCOTLAND YARD
BARONESS EMMA ORCZY

DETECTIVES 4

BROMLEY BARNES
GEORGE BARTON

TRENT'S LAST CASE
E. C. BENTLEY

KALA PERSAD
HEADON HILL

GALLAGHER
RICHARD HARDING DAVIS

DETECTIVES 3

AN ARISTOCRATIC DETECTIVE
RICHARD MARSH

JANE SPROOD, DETECTIVE
ELLIS PARKER BUTLER

THE DELIBERATE DETECTIVE
E. PHILLIPS OPPENHEIM

www.ingramcontent.com/pod-product-compliance
Lightning Source LLC
Chambersburg PA
CBHW050532260626
47157CB00004B/1572

* 9 7 8 1 6 1 6 4 6 4 9 8 1 *